SHADES

by
Zoey Daly

Contents

Prologue

Allie Kate Shadowbridge lay in her crib the night before her first birthday, the soft glow of the moon casting gentle shadows on the walls. The air was still, wrapped in a blanket of quiet. Outside her window, a figure—something beyond human—moved with an eerie grace, its shape shifting in the dim light. A shiver ran through the room, though the baby remained blissfully unaware of the mystery that loomed just beyond her dreams.

Then the ticking of the clock stopped, and the wind in the trees fell silent, as if time itself had frozen. Without warning, the creature outside burst through the window, a dark figure cloaked in shadows. A black mist seeped from the floor, wrapping around the room like a serpent, its chill as biting as the Arctic, creeping toward the baby. Allie Kate stirred, a shudder passing through her tiny body, as if sensing the encroaching darkness.

"Halt."

The mist stirred no more.

"This child will do well in the future—as long as I keep her for myself." The voice emerged from the figure, its red eyes glowing like embers in the dark. "There is nothing special about this one, despite what He insists. That is why we must keep her... safe." The last word dripped with disgust, a low chuckle accompanying it, sending a shiver through the room.

As the creature loomed closer, Allie Kate instinctively curled up, sensing the darkness enveloping her, though she remained blissfully unaware of the true danger.

"But ssir, you ssaid the girl is nothing sspecial. Why bother?" A massive snake, as long as a truck and as thick as a tree trunk, slithered from beneath the mist, wrapping around the crib to peer down at Allie Kate.

"Quiet, Siege. Don't worry. She will remember this night quite differently." The figure's voice was smooth but laced with menace. "Now go. Gather my focus and meet me at the castle. Tonight, we celebrate. Tonight, we celebrate the nearing of His defeat."

The snake flicked its tongue, tasting the air, before slithering away, leaving a lingering chill in its wake.

As soon as he left, the first figure leaned closer, murmuring words that no one could understand. Bright lights suddenly spun around Allie, their intensity burning her delicate skin. They pulsed with energy, soaking into her, leaving a searing sensation in their wake. Just as quickly as they appeared, everything went black.

Chapter 1

"Okay, class. The bell will ring in ten minutes, and I want you all finished picking your animal by then," Mrs. Rosemary repeated for what felt like the umpteenth time.

At the last minute, Mrs. Rosemary had asked the class to suggest animals for next year's project, not wanting to do it herself.

The students exchanged glances—some excited, others groaning at the last-minute task. Allie felt a mix of anticipation and uncertainty. What animal would she choose?

Allie looked over at her best friend, Stella Waterbrook, who was focused on sketching an animal in her notebook.

"She's talking to you, you know," Stella said with a smile, her eyes still on the page.

Allie sighed. "I know."

Allie glanced at Stella's notebook again. Stella was always the best in art class, and Allie couldn't remember a day she'd seen her without her sketchbook.

With a sigh, Allie raised her hand.

"Yes, Allie," Mrs. Rosemary said, finally noticing the hand she'd been looking for.

"Can I still pick the eagle?" Allie asked.

"Yes, you sure can. Is that the animal you want?" Mrs. Rosemary asked, her hopeful tone echoing in the room. As Allie glanced around at her classmates, she wished she had picked an animal sooner.

Everyone was looking at her, knowing they'd be let out of school—"prison," as they were calling it—early if she picked an animal. When she finally did, a cheer erupted, and bags were hurriedly rummaged as everyone rushed for the door.

"Yes, that'll be my pick," she responded, even though the class had already taken it as a yes.

"Great, Allie! Excuse me, class! I know I said you'd be let out early, but we have two minutes left, and I need to share some important information."

A loud groan rose from the class as everyone reluctantly sat back down.

As Mrs. Rosemary gave announcements and passed out last-minute graded papers, Allie's mind drifted away, thinking about the eagle.

She kept daydreaming until, suddenly, she felt like someone was tickling her all over. But no one was. It was like the tingling sensation when your hand falls asleep. *What is that?*

"Great! Class dismissed."

"Have a wonderful summer break, everyone! See you next year," Mrs. Rosemary called as her class poured out of the room like dying animals racing toward a watering hole.

"Come on, Allie! You're so slow! Let's make tomorrow come faster," Stella called impatiently from the door.

"Coming!" Allie replied quickly, trying to stuff her papers into her backpack without crushing them. They were having a sleepover the next night, and both their moms had agreed on it, wanting the girls to enjoy a good night's sleep in their own beds now that school was over. The girls thought it was completely unnecessary.

Apparently, Allie had been packing too slowly for Stella. She rushed over to Allie's desk and pulled her out the door. Allie laughed as she tried to break free.

"Wait! I still have to grab my stuff!" she exclaimed.

I'll deal with the weird feelings later, she thought.

Both Allie and Stella lived in the charming small town of Willowston. Allie's house was on the edge of a state park, surrounded by about five acres of land. Stella lived down the street, just two miles from Dolphin Beach. The girls loved spending time there together.

"See you tomorrow!" Allie called back to Stella as she hopped out of the car, landing at the end of their long gravel driveway. "Oh, and thank you for driving me all year, Mrs. Waterbrook."

"You're welcome, sweetie," Stella's mom replied.

"See ya tomorrow, Allie!"

As Allie walked down the path to her house, something stirred in the trees, but she was too caught up in the excitement of summer to notice. The woods felt peaceful around her. A family of bunnies darted across the path, and a baby eagle flapped its wings in a nest above.

"Eagles! I can't wait to see what the projects look like next year. That baby eagle is adorable! I'm really looking forward to when it starts flying."

"Ow!" Allie yelped.

There it was again—the tingling sensation. This time, with no distractions, it felt more intense and lingered longer. Though it was only the second occurrence, Allie felt a mix of curiosity and fear about what was happening. It was as if she vaguely remembered something similar from before, but the memory was just out of reach. Determined to uncover the truth, she resolved to figure it out soon.

At dinner, her parents insisted she share everything she'd done at school that day. One of the many reasons Allie was glad summer had started was that she wouldn't have to recite her day anymore. After they pried out every last detail, the conversation shifted to the sprinkler guy who hadn't shown up that day.

Allie looked down, fiddling with the meatball on her plate, tuning out their conversation. She had skipped mentioning the strange feeling she'd experienced at the end of school; she wasn't sure how to explain it.

She also knew she wanted to understand what had happened at school—was it real, or could it have been just her imagination?

"Allie."

Startled, she looked up at her parents. "Yes?"

Mrs. Shadowbridge paused, fixing her gaze on Allie. "We didn't say anything, honey."

"But I just heard—"

"Allie."

She stood up so quickly she almost knocked the table over. "Someone is saying my name!" Allie said, looking around.

"Allie. No one is saying your name. Now, If you are done with dinner, go get ready for bed. I think you are just tired." Mr. Shadowbridge sighed, getting up to clear the plates.

"Ugh," Allie muttered quietly as she headed upstairs. She couldn't shake the feeling of disbelief. How could her parents not believe her?

If they don't believe me about the voice, they won't believe me about that weird feeling, she thought, frustrated. With a grunt, she walked into the bathroom and turned on the water to brush her teeth.

"Good night, Allie," her mom said as she tucked her in. But Allie's mind was far from sleep.

"Night, Mom," she replied, stifling a yawn and hoping to nudge her mom toward the door. Allie had a plan. At midnight, she would sneak out to the clearing in the woods.

Since all the strange occurrences began when she thought about eagles, Allie decided to focus on that and see what would happen. She didn't expect anything to come of it. As she lay in bed, she tried to convince herself that this was just her imagination and that magic—if that's what it was—wasn't real. But no matter how hard she tried, she couldn't shake the feeling of being drawn into the forest. It was as if something was summoning her there.

"See you in the morning, sweet pea," her mother said as she closed the door, finally leaving the room. The waiting began.

Tick tock. Tock tock. Tick tock. Minute after minute crawled by as Allie stared at her clock. It felt like years until, at last, the hands finally reached midnight.

Allie slowly crept out of bed, putting on her coat and shoes before sneaking out of the house as quietly as possible. When she reached the clearing in the woods, she paused. *What am I doing? This is ridiculous. Probably nothing will happen. I'm just kidding myself.* Yet the pull she felt was undeniable.

Allie focused on everything she could think of about eagles. At first, nothing happened. *I knew this was stupid.* But then the sensation began, spreading through her body, shifting from a slight tingling to an intense pain.

Stop! Please stop! Allie screamed in her head. The pain was unlike anything she had ever imagined, as if a thousand swords were stabbing her. It was so overwhelming that she couldn't even open her mouth to scream. Time felt frozen, every moment stretching into eternity.

Then, just a second later, the pain stopped. Collapsing onto the lush forest floor, Allie finally relaxed.

"Ahh." She looked down at her body, feeling her face to check for any signs of bleeding. She could have sworn she felt it, but there was none to be seen.

As the strange sensation returned, Allie instinctively reached up to touch her nose. Something's not right! It felt hard and sharp.

Jumping to her feet, Allie raced home. She quietly slipped through her bedroom window, turned on the light, and hurried to the mirror.

It took every ounce of willpower not to scream when she saw her reflection. Instead of a nose and mouth, she had a beak.

Chapter 2

Allie was pacing her room the next morning when her dad called from outside the door. "Allie, your mom wants you downstairs for breakfast."

"Dad, can you tell her I'm not hungry? Please? I'm not feeling well, and I think I'll stay in my room all day." She continued pacing.

"Are you sure? Can I come in to check on you?"

"NO!" Allie replied a bit too quickly, then paused, finally facing the door. "I mean, no, please. I'll be fine later—just not right now."

"Okay, I'll go tell Mom." To Allie's relief, she heard her dad head downstairs. But a few minutes later, he reappeared.

"Allie," he said, "Mom insists you come down for breakfast."

She grabbed a hoodie and, with anxious thoughts swirling in her mind, slowly made her way downstairs.

Relief washed over her when she saw the kitchen was empty. She quickly grabbed some food and hurried back upstairs.

She took a deep breath and flopped down on her bed. Allie knew she would have to leave her room eventually, and she might not be so lucky to avoid her parents that time. She remembered how they had reacted when she mentioned hearing that voice, but this was a whole new level.

Allie was also terrified about the sleepover that night with Stella. How was she going to sneak into the woods again? More importantly, how would Stella react? Stella had always been her best friend, and when they were six, they had promised to stick together through hard times. But their six-year-old minds hadn't considered anything like this.

Several hours later, Mrs. Shadowbridge knocked on Allie's door.

"Allie, how are you feeling? You've been locked up in your room most of the day. Are you ready to get up?"

Ugh, MOM! "Nope, everything's great!" Allie lied. She hated lying to her mom, but she couldn't figure out what else to say.

"Yes, Mom. Something is wrong. I snuck out last night and ended up with an eagle's beak. I just don't know why or how to get rid of it."

Allie peeked out her door and glanced down the stairs. Her mom was in the kitchen, starting on bacon. She wouldn't be upstairs anytime soon. Without wasting another moment, Allie crawled out her window and sprinted toward the woods.

"AHHHHHHH!" she screamed into the woods, wondering how no one had heard her. Upset, angry, and confused, she didn't know what else to do.

"Allie."

This time, she didn't even bother searching for the source of the voice.

No one in my family would understand. I can't even grasp what was happening myself, and I can't tell them—they'd just freak out. The only person I could confide in is my big brother, Jacob, but he is away at college.

She looked up and noticed an eagle soaring above her. *No, not an eagle!* It circled and circled overhead, almost as if it were hunting her as its prey. Then, as if sensing her thoughts, it suddenly flew away.

Sigh. Allie sank down onto the grass, leaning her head against the tree trunk as she took a shaky breath. She had never felt so overwhelmed—not even during the end-of-year tests at school. She reached up to pull her hood off but froze when she noticed something falling around her. Shreds of fabric piled up on the grass as her ripped hood finally slipped free, landing in her lap. She looked down at her hands—and realized they weren't hands at all; they were eagle talons!

Tears streamed down her face, amplifying her confusion. Leaving the fabric on the ground, she jumped up and ran home, sneaking through her window. She did her best not to break her computer as she ordered thick gloves and a pack of new hoodies, sensing that she would need more soon.

That evening, Stella arrived.

Ding dong. "Oh, come on in, Stella," Mrs. Shadowbridge said. "Allie's up in her room and hasn't been acting like herself today."

You have no idea, Allie thought, listening to the conversation from her room.

"Do you mind seeing if she'll come down? She's not really letting anyone into her room."

"Sure thing, Mrs. Shadowbridge," Stella replied, bringing in her duffle bag and sleeping bag.

Mrs. Shadowbridge disappeared back into the kitchen.

"Oh, Stella. Hi! Can you give this to Allie? It just came in," Mr. Shadowbridge said, handing her a large box.

"Yes, sir," Stella replied, stifling a laugh as everything tumbled to the ground when she tried to grab the box. "I'll get everything up there eventually."

"Do you need any help?" Mr. Shadowbridge asked.

"Nah, thanks, though," Stella replied as she climbed the stairs. She had finally figured out how to balance everything.

Knock, knock. Allie stood behind the door, opening it just enough so Stella wouldn't see her.

"Put the box inside," she said quietly, then quickly shut the door before Stella could step in.

"O-k...," Stella said, and Allie could hear the uncertainty in her voice.

With great anticipation, Allie opened the box. Inside were the gloves and hoodies. She quickly put them on, slid the box under the bed, and sat down across from the door.

"Come in. Quickly," Allie called in a loud whisper once she was situated.

Stella entered, shut the door behind her, and dumped all her stuff on the floor before sitting down in the desk chair.

"Allie, what's going on?" Stella asked, her eyes widening at what Allie was wearing.

Sigh. Allie had known from the start that, under the circumstances, it was going to be a challenging night.

Allie trusted Stella—she was her best friend. But her concern lingered: she didn't know how Stella would react. In fact, she had no idea how anyone would respond.

I'm so glad this is happening over the summer and not during the school year, Allie thought.

"Something's happened," she said, her voice barely above a whisper.

"What?" Stella whispered, leaning forward in the desk chair.

"I don't know," Allie said, slightly irritated. "Something really bad has happened to me, and I don't want to talk about it. Just draw something, okay? I'll be right back." Allie hurried toward the door.

"Allie, don't shut me out. What happened? It can't be that bad," Stella said, trying to lighten the mood with a light laugh.

Allie appreciated the effort, but it only made her angrier.

"Does this look bad to you?" Allie spun around, tearing off the gloves and hoodie, shredding them in the process. When she finished, the remnants lay scattered around her. She took a deep breath as her newly grown beak and claws were revealed to Stella.

After a few moments of silence, Allie slowly looked up at Stella. She was sitting there with her mouth agape, just staring. Eventually, though, Stella found her voice.

"H... how? Wh... what?" Stella stammered.

Allie walked over to the box and grabbed another pair of gloves and a fresh hoodie. But halfway through putting them on, Stella stopped her.

"Allie, what happened?" Stella asked, her voice tinged with nervousness.

"I don't know how to explain it. Every time I think about eagles, it feels like I'm being attacked by a swarm of killer bees. At first, I just had a beak, but then these claws appeared. I don't know what to do."

Stella fell silent for a moment. She walked over to her bag on the floor, unzipped it, and pulled out her sketchbook. Then she returned to the desk and sat down with her back to Allie.

I knew it. She thinks I'm crazy, Allie thought as she pulled her hoodie and gloves back on and sat down on her bed.

Allie had heard of shapeshifting before. Was that what was happening to her? When would her beak and claws go away? And most importantly, what had caused this in the first place?

The room was quiet for a moment, except for the sound of Stella's pencil scratching on paper.

"Are you going to try again?" Stella asked quietly.

Allie looked up and tilted her head slightly. "I wasn't planning to."

"Maybe you should try right now." Stella's full attention remained on her sketchbook.

As Stella continued sketching, Allie began to share her questions. After all, she was her best friend—shouldn't friends trust each other?

Stella listened intently to Allie's concerns. Together, they began to formulate a plan.

Chapter 3

The next morning, Stella covered for Allie all day, bringing her food so she wouldn't have to leave her room. After dinner, Stella went home. Later that night, at midnight, they met outside Allie's house, ready to head into the forest according to their plan.

Stella had insisted that Allie leave behind the hoodie and gloves, convincing her there was no one around to see. Reluctantly, Allie agreed.

"You ready?" Stella asked as they moved out of sight from the house.

"No, not really. I'm not sure if I'm more terrified of being attacked by those killer bees again or excited to see what happens next." Allie gave a half-hearted laugh.

"I'd be excited if I were you," Stella said, walking a little ahead and holding up a low-hanging tree branch for Allie to pass under. "Wow! This is totally awesome! Just think—if you had a superpower like shapeshifting, wouldn't you want to find out what it could do?" She looked back at Allie, her eyes sparkling with enthusiasm.

"I don't know. It's hard enough getting out of bed with two legs. Imagine if I turned into an octopus and had to get up with eight." Allie said in a matter-of-fact tone, but her delivery made Stella burst into laughter.

They turned the corner and entered the clearing at last. The light from the nearly full moon was the only illumination on the grass, aside from the beams from the flashlights that Allie and Stella carried.

"Okay." Stella sat down on a tree stump while Allie stood in the middle of the clearing. "I think we're ready."

As Allie began to think about eagles, the pain surged back, enveloping her entire body. It felt like she was on fire! It was a struggle not to scream for her mind to stop.

"Stella?" Allie asked, her voice rising in pitch. "Stella?" Allie asked, her voice getting higher.

"It's okay!" Stella called from the ground. "I think," she added under her breath.

Allie was suspended in the air for what felt like hours. She quickly became enveloped in a ball of light, making it impossible for Stella to look at her. The next thing Allie knew, she felt herself crash to the ground.

"Ow," Allie said. When she looked up, Stella was staring at her.

Stella was certain she was hallucinating. She closed her eyes, shook her head, and then looked at Allie again.

"Hold on." Stella pulled out her phone and snapped a picture of Allie. Then she slowly turned the screen to face her.

Allie was an eagle.

They stared at the picture for what felt like an eternity.

I'm an eagle! I really look like an eagle! There's absolutely no resemblance to a human at all! Allie flapped her wings and was surprised by how easily she lifted off the ground. With two powerful strokes, she soared into the air. But then, a thought suddenly struck her.

"How am I going to change back?" Allie asked, landing and folding her wings.

"You tell me! I'm not an expert at... whatever this is." Stella's voice was a mix of shock and fascination.

That was easier said than done. The realization that neither of them had any idea how to change her back hit Allie like a boulder.

"Why don't we go back to the house and think it through there?" Stella suggested. She had been gently examining Allie's wings, marveling at every little detail.

"Okay. Yeah, sure." Allie was still in shock about what would happen next and took off without thinking. By the time Stella reached the house, Allie was perched on her windowsill.

Once they were back, Stella and Allie spent the rest of the morning trying to figure out what had happened and why. But no matter how many times they reviewed the events, they kept arriving at the same answers—and even more questions.

"Okay, so I thought of an eagle and turned into one, with no explanation whatsoever," Allie reiterated.

"Yes," Stella replied, sitting cross-legged on Allie's bed with her sketchbook in her lap.

"What are you drawing?" Allie asked, finally giving up on her dilemma for the first time in five hours.

Allie flew up and landed on her bed next to Stella, peering over her shoulder to see the sketchbook. Stella was drawing Allie! One half of her was human, while the other half was an eagle.

"I started this when you first told me what was happening. I didn't think about what would come of it; I just thought it would make a cool drawing. But as it turns out, I was right! I had to make the eagle a lot bigger than usual to match the proportions of a human. What do you think? Is it turning out okay?" she asked Allie.

"Yeah," Allie breathed. It truly looked amazing. Stella had blended the lines of the eagle feathers and Allie's body together so well that it really looked like they were one.

"Allie! Breakfast!" Mrs. Shadowbridge called from the doorway, making Allie jump. She dove under the bed just before her mom opened the door.

The girls hadn't even realized how late it had gotten.

"Goodness, I didn't mean to scare you. Stella, when did you get here?"

"Oh..."

Stella sat there feeling very exposed. How was she going to explain being in Allie's room?

"I just popped in when you didn't answer the door and came on up."

"The door was open, probably from when Mrs. Shadowbridge left for work."

"All right then. Wait, where is Allie?" Mrs. Shadowbridge asked.

Great.

"She's hiding," Stella said simply. At least that much was true. Allie's eyes shone with gratitude toward Stella from under the bed.

"Okay, have fun," Mrs. Shadowbridge said as she left the room. "But you better find her. Breakfast is in ten minutes." She shut the door with a wink.

Once Allie was sure her mom was downstairs, she slowly crawled out from under the bed, trying not to hurt her wings.

"That was close," Stella said, lying on her back. "Does she always make you jump?"

"Yup. I'm surprised I'm not used to it." Allie laughed despite the circumstances, but Stella remained quiet.

"What is it?" Allie asked.

"I wonder if thinking about your human self will turn you back, just like you transformed into an eagle when you focused on that. I mean, if this is a superpower, you should be able to control it, right?"

Allie paused, deep in thought. It made sense, and they needed to figure it out soon—she couldn't go down to breakfast like this! "Worth a shot."

Allie began to imagine herself as a human. The sensation started, but this time it didn't hurt as much. She felt herself changing until Stella gasped again. Allie opened her eyes and looked into the mirror.

She was human again! No more claws, no more beak, no more wings. Overjoyed, she ran to hug Stella. "Thank you!"

But the relief was short-lived; the confusion still lingered for both of them.

Chapter 4

Before Stella left that morning after breakfast, the girls decided it would be a good idea for Allie to try shapeshifting into an eagle again. Although Allie was unsure why it was necessary, Stella found a way to convince her to give it a shot.

If it worked, she planned to try turning into other animals as well. So, when Stella left, Allie asked her mom if she could go to the clearing. Once her mom said yes, she set out on her mission.

This time, when she arrived at the clearing, Allie made sure to bring a mirror so she could see when her transformation was complete. She set the mirror against a tree and stood in the center of the clearing. Then, in her mind, she declared, "Turn into an eagle."

Allie felt herself change, and this time there was almost no pain at all—it took only about 30 seconds. The process was getting faster. Stella had been right; she had discovered a way to make shapeshifting smoother. By simply focusing on the animal or human she wanted to become, Allie could control the transformation much more easily. Excitement bubbled within her as she reveled in the thrill of her new abilities. This was just the beginning of her adventure!

Before Allie could think of anything else, she heard her mom calling her in for lunch. Once again, she had lost track of time. With a quick determination, she shifted back to her human form and promised herself to return to the clearing at midnight.

As bedtime approached, Allie felt torn between her desire to head to the clearing and the need for sleep. She set her alarm for 11:45 and, after an hour of tossing and turning, finally drifted off. Yet, the sleep she found was anything but peaceful.

Allie dreamed she was a baby, nestled in a field of vibrant flowers. Suddenly, a creature with red eyes emerged from the ground, its presence accompanied by a thick, black mist that withered the blossoms around her. It spoke in a language no one could comprehend, while brilliant lights whirled around her, searing her skin with their touch.

Then the lights soaked into her skin and when they were gone everything went black.

Allie woke up an hour before her alarm, panting and sweating. Her heart slowed as she realized it was just a dream and that she was in her bed safe. But she had a weird feeling that she was going to see those red eyes again.

Unable to fall back asleep, Allie got up and headed to the clearing to practice shapeshifting and clear her mind. She transformed into an eagle and back again, repeating the motion until, eventually, she found herself no longer hurting in her transformations, nor could she see any light around her.

Allie continued practicing until the transformation occurred in the blink of an eye. Then she remembered Stella's other challenge: to see if she could shapeshift into something else. She chose the first animal that came to mind and said, "Turn into a fox." Almost instantly, she felt the transformation begin.

A moment later, she glanced into the mirror—and yes! She was a fox! She could shapeshift into anything! The fact that she had transformed into both an eagle and a fox so quickly made her believe that shapeshifting would soon feel like second nature.

Suddenly she noticed that the sun was starting to rise. *Oh no! Mom and dad will be wondering where I am!*

People say that fear gives you adrenaline and that night, Allie understood why. She had barely practiced but already knew what to do.

Allie transformed into a cheetah and sprinted home as fast as she could. When she reached her window, she shifted into a monkey and swung into her room. Once inside, she transformed back into herself, just as she heard her dad approaching the door.

"Time for breakfast!" Mr. Shadowbridge called with a grin as he leaned into Allie's bedroom. "Mom made pancakes!"

Allie pulled herself out of bed, feigning sleepiness, but she was actually buzzing with excitement about calling Stella after breakfast to share her incredible discovery.

"Dad, can Stella come over for a sleepover tonight?" she blurted, jumping out of bed and completely forgetting her act.

Mr. Shadowbridge raised an eyebrow. "Didn't you just have one?"

"All right, yes, but it's summer! I was hoping we could camp out in the clearing." Allie could see her dad weighing the idea, considering her enthusiasm.

"Actually, that's a great idea! We could have a family campout—get the Waterbrooks and the Shadowbridges together. Let me go talk to your mom about it." With that, he left the room before Allie could respond.

It's fine. I'll find a way to show her. Although that hadn't been her original plan, Allie felt confident she could reveal her new discovery to Stella. Plus, the idea of the campout made her a little giddy with excitement.

"So, what did you want to show me?" Stella asked. Their families had agreed to the campout, and Allie had found a way to talk to Stella alone.

"Umm, name a random animal," Allie said, trying to sound casual.

"Alligator," Stella replied slowly, clearly unsure of where this was headed.

Oh, good! That's a new one! Okay, turn into an alligator. Thankfully, Allie's transformations now happened in the blink of an eye; otherwise, she might have shown signs of an alligator before she fully transformed.

Allie opened her eyes as soon as she heard Stella let out a little scream. *Turn into me!*

As soon as Allie transformed back, she ran over to her. "It's okay, Stella! It was me." But Stella didn't look convinced.

"I promise," Allie said, hoping she hadn't made a mistake by showing her. She was surprised by Stella's reaction, especially after how brave she'd seemed the night before.

"I thought you could only turn into an eagle. Wait—you can turn into anything, can't you?" Stella gasped, her eyes wide with astonishment.

"Yes! Stella, you were right! Now all we have to figure out is why," Allie said, smiling. That was going to be the hard part. Ignoring her parents' constant questions was one thing, but doing research on her new abilities would be much trickier.

"Well, come on! Let's get this off our shoulders. We're having s'mores next! Maybe that will help us think!" They both laughed and ran toward the delicious smell of melting chocolate and toasted marshmallows.

Later that night, after s'mores, everyone gathered for their favorite campfire tradition: scary stories. Allie felt a thrill of excitement—it was Mr. Shadowbridge's turn, and in her opinion, he always told the best ones.

"It's time I tell you all the legend of Sephtis!" he began, slipping into his spooky storytelling voice.

"Many years ago, when this forest stretched for miles, explorers came to assess the land for colonization. One glance at these beautiful woods gave them their answer. But as they began making their building plans, a thick mist rolled in from nowhere. Then, out of the shadows, a creature emerged."

This sounds familiar... Allie thought,

"A black and gray lion with piercing red eyes and a mane of flickering black fire emerged from the mist. In a slow, deep, threatening voice, he declared himself Sephtis, the king of the world and the guardian of the portal hidden in these woods. He warned the explorers they could stay, but only on one condition."

"Somewhere down your line of generations, a child will accept my punishment for trespassing on sacred ground. That child will possess abilities beyond your wildest imagination, and they will be forced to serve me forever," Sephtis said, a devious grin spreading across his face.

"There is one exception, however," Sephtis said slowly. "If the child can find the portal and locate me before their fourteenth birthday, they will have the choice to avoid becoming my property forever." With that, he vanished into the mist, never to be seen again," Mr. Shadowbridge concluded.

When her father finished, he glanced around at everyone with a smile. After a moment of silence, nervous laughter erupted around the campfire.

"I remember Dad telling us a story just like this! He always tried to scare us before bed," one of Stella's older brothers chimed in.

Allie looked up at her father, a mix of excitement and dread swelling inside her. He had no idea how real this story was about to become.

"Dad, where did you hear this story?" Allie asked, her voice shaking slightly.

"Oh, my grandfather—your great-great-grandfather—told me this when I was about your age. He always warned me not to underestimate it," Dad replied, trying to catch his breath along with everyone else.

The only other person around the campfire who hadn't laughed was Stella. She caught Allie's eye and gave her a knowing look. They both understood what that meant.

Yup, I was right. This story is about me! I'm the child. I'm the one with powers beyond their wildest imagination! I'm going to become like Sephtis! Allie couldn't bear everyone's carefree reactions any longer.

"Excuse me for a moment." Allie needed to clear her head. As soon as she was out of sight, she started running—she didn't know where, but she couldn't stop.

Chapter 5

Allie had been running for a while and was starting to tire. She sank onto a tree stump to collect her thoughts. Now her dream made sense. *I have to find Sephtis. Soon. But how?* She could hardly believe any of this was true in the first place.

"Allie, I found you! You know what this story means, right?" Stella emerged from nowhere, causing Allie to jump off the stump and trip over a log—all in about three seconds.

"Oh, are you okay?" Stella asked, noticing Allie's tear-stained face.

"No. Stella, it's true—it's all true," Allie said slowly, sinking down into the grass.

"Okay, that answers my question." Stella sat down next to her on the ground. "So, what do we do now?"

"We?" Allie asked, propping herself up on her elbows, surprise evident in her voice.

"Yes, we're in this together. No way am I letting my best friend take this on by herself. So, what are we going to do first?" Stella's voice brimmed with determination, and Allie could tell she meant every word.

"Umm," Allie paused to think. "I guess the first thing we need to do is gather as much information about Sephtis as possible. I just wish I knew how." She said this with a hint of sadness in her voice.

A moment of silence hung between them.

"What if you asked your grandpa? Since your dad got the story from his grandfather, maybe he shared it with his son and grandson too," Stella suggested.

While Stella was speaking, Allie was also forming a plan in her mind. She quickly built on what Stella had said and turned to face her.

"That's a great idea! Okay, I've got a plan. You gather as much information as you can by going through the story my dad told us. Maybe even check the library to see if they have other versions with more details. Meanwhile, I'll talk to my grandpa and see if I can find anything from him. How does that sound?" Allie said excitedly.

"Sounds good. But we should probably head back to the campsite before our parents start to worry," Stella suggested.

Allie had completely forgotten about that. "Oh, right! That's a good idea too." She tried to laugh, but it came out weak. Without another word, they ran back to the campsite in silence.

The next day, Allie went to her grandparents' house, which was just two blocks away, so she didn't need to worry about asking her parents for a ride.

"Well, we weren't expecting you!" Grandma exclaimed when her granddaughter knocked on the door. "Come on in, sweetie. You're just in time for tea. I'll put the kettle on," she said as she headed to the kitchen.

"Hi, Grandma. Sorry, I can't stay long today. I came to ask Grandpa a few questions. I'm gathering some campfire stories for a slumber party I'm having soon." Allie explained.

"Oh, he's in his office, honey. Just let me know if you'd like any tea," Grandma said.

"Thank you, I will." Allie walked over to the office and found her grandfather sitting at his art desk.

"Hi, Grandpa. Do you mind if I ask you a few questions?" she asked, trying to be quick without seeming rude.

"Oh, hi Allie! Of course. You are just like me. Get straight to the point as I always say. Well now, let me just go wash this brush and then we can talk." he said as he was getting up.

When he left, Allie took two chairs from the table and placed them facing each other. She sat down in one and waited for him to return. He came back a few minutes later.

"Ok what questions do you have for me?" Grandpa asked with a smile.

"'Well, it's about a campfire story my dad told us last night. Umm, the one about Sephtis."

"Yes, that one," her grandfather replied. "It's one of my favorite campfire stories."

"Right. I have, um… a few questions about it. First, does the legend mention anything about how to find Sephtis or the portal?" Allie asked.

"In fact, it does!" Grandpa said. "The legend states that you can find the portal by following the sun as it sets in the west. However, the portal is only open and visible to the human eye under a full moon at midnight. Why? Are you trying to get to the Pertiaus Realm?" he asked.

She quickly wrote that down. "Wait. The Pertiaus Realm?" She paused her writing.

"Yes. That is the name of the realm you would enter if you went through the portal," Grandpa revealed slowly.

"Nice." That detail wasn't really important to her at the moment. "What about finding Sephtis?" she asked again.

"All I know is that he lives on the other side of the portal, in the Shadow of the Moon," Grandpa answered.

Allie quickly scribbled that down.

"Okay, last thing. Um… has there ever been any rumors that the spell on the child has already been cast and is no longer a threat?" Allie asked.

"No, actually. Sephtis's enchantment still looms over mankind," Grandpa said with a wink.

Allie tried to laugh.

"Well, thank you so much. This has been really helpful, but I should get going," Allie said as she hopped up.

"Oh, are you sure? You've only just arrived. And I just heard Alice put the kettle on for tea," he said, looking visibly disappointed.

"No, I'm afraid I can't stay. I promised Stella I'd meet her at the library," Allie replied.

"Of course. Just promise me you'll come back and visit us soon," he said, just as her grandmother entered the room.

"Okay, dear, the kettle is ready and so is the tea," Grandma exclaimed.

"Well, I'm sorry, but I really have to go. That's all the time I have for today," Allie said, still trying to make her exit.

"I'm sorry to hear that, dear. Well, come on, I'll show you out," Grandma said.

Allie began to follow her, but just as they rounded the corner, her grandpa called for her again.

"Allie, just remember... magic isn't real. This could all just be a dream," he said, looking worried for some reason.

Allie smiled at him. "Sure, Grandpa."

She quickly turned and hurried out the door before he could call her back. Allie couldn't wait to share what she had learned with Stella and find out if Stella had discovered anything. She was ready to find Sephtis and put an end to this.

Chapter 6

Stella, sitting alone, was in a section of the library that neither she nor Allie had seen before. But that wasn't surprising—their library had three stories. The first floor was the children's section, the second was for adult nonfiction, and the third housed the adult fiction collection.

The section of the library where Stella sat was a large, circular room. The only light came from a grand chandelier in the center, casting a glow over a large round table beneath it. The door to the room was labeled 'Tales and Legends.'

She had notes spread out across the entire table, surrounded by books and notepaper. Stella was once again poring over a book titled 'Old Legends.' Just as she was about to give up, text Allie to meet at her house and call it a day, she hesitated.

"Hey, I see you found a lot on... our subject," Allie said as she sat down in the chair next to Stella. She was about to mention her power when she noticed the librarian walking into the room.

"Huh, oh hi! Yeah, it turns out they—" But Stella stopped when Allie placed a finger to her lips and nodded toward the librarian, who was now shelving books.

"They must have at least twenty versions of that campfire story," Stella whispered, her voice low and conspiratorial. "I went through every single one and pieced together this information about the spell and Sephtis." She slid a sheet of paper toward Allie, covered in scribbled notes. Two sections, in particular, caught Allie's eye:

<u>Spell:</u>
<u>Potential Powers:</u>
<u>Fire control</u>
<u>Water control</u>
<u>Shape-shifting</u>
<u>Flying</u>
<u>Levitation</u>

<u>Sephtis:</u>
<u>Resides in the Shadow of the Moon</u>

"That's great, but what about all of these?" Allie gestured to the pile of papers scattered across the table.

"They were here when I got here," Stella replied, glancing at the mess.

"Oh... right. But if we make it to the other side of the portal, how will we know what the Shadow of the Moon is?" Allie asked, her voice uncertain.

"Oh, I almost forgot to show you this!" Stella exclaimed, pulling out an old, hand-drawn map and handing it to Allie. "It fell out of one of the books when I took it off the shelf."

Allie studied the map while Stella continued, her voice brimming with excitement. "I couldn't find this place anywhere on the globe, so I checked the books—and guess what? One of them had the exact same map on a page! Allie, I think this is a map to the other side of the portal!"

Allie examined the map closely. The handwriting was nearly illegible, but she could make out a few words.

"Lake of Memories? Misty Meadows? I've never heard of those," she muttered.

This must be the Pertiaus Realm, she thought to herself.

As Allie continued examining the map, the librarian entered the room again. Her eyes scanned the page until something at the bottom caught her attention. It read: Portal.

"Stella," Allie whispered, pointing at the map. "Look."

Silence.

"This confirms everything. We need to leave as soon as possible."

Allie spoke quietly. Stella began gathering the books, carefully dodging the librarian, who seemed in no hurry to leave. Allie was just about to say something when Stella suddenly sat back down.

"Wait, I'm sorry. I haven't even heard what you found," she said, looking at Allie expectantly.

"Oh, right," Allie said, then began explaining everything she had written down.

"So, to find the portal, we have to 'follow the sun as it sets in the west,' and Sephtis lives in the Shadow of the Moon. Well, we already knew that," Stella sighed.

"Yes, and this place is called the Pertiaus Realm," Allie said, still focused on the map while Stella skimmed her notes.

"Wait, repeat the last part," Allie asked.

"Follow the sun?"

"No, the other one—the part about Sephtis."

"Oh, he lives in the Shadow of the Moon," Stella repeated.

Shadow of the Moon. Shadow of the Moon, Allie thought, certain she had seen something like that on the map.

There! Her eyes locked onto the spot.

"Stella, look at the Snow Cap Peaks! It's the Shadow of the Moon!" Allie exclaimed.

As soon as Stella saw it, she turned to Allie.

"Sephtis!" they both said in unison.

"Alright, your fourteenth birthday is in a week. So, in seven days, we need to: find the hidden portal, track down Sephtis, and ask him to lift his enchantment," Stella said. It sounded like an impossible task to both of them.

Allie took a deep breath. "Okay, we'll gather everything we need today and meet in the clearing at eleven-thirty tonight. Sounds good?" she asked, trying to hide the mix of fear and excitement in her voice.

"Perfect." She said simply, "See you then."

They put up all the books and checked out the map from the library. Then they both went straight home.

Allie pretended to be asleep when her parents came in to say goodnight. As soon as they left the room, she got up and turned on the light. She pulled out her hiking backpack and began packing.

Her dad had always told her to lay everything out before packing it into a bag or suitcase to ensure she had everything she needed. There was no way Allie was going to forget that advice tonight.

"Rope, water, map, snacks, hiking boots, headlamp, phone fully charged with tracking turned off and a solar-powered attachment, my solar charging watch, grappling hook, compass, coordinates tracker…" Allie paused, thinking. *Umm, what else?* "Oh! First aid kit and sleeping mat!" She added those to her pile. *I think I have everything.*

She packed everything into her bag, then turned off the light and approached the window. Just as she was about to climb out, she noticed a picture of her family on the windowsill. She grabbed it, slipped it into her backpack, and then jumped down to the ground. She might want that in the days to come.

Chapter 7

Allie arrived at the clearing thirty minutes early, eager to gather her thoughts before Stella showed up. She settled onto a weathered stump, taking a moment to reflect on everything swirling in her mind.

Thump. Thump. The sound of fast-approaching footsteps echoed through the air. Thump. Thump. Heart racing, Allie ducked behind the stump. Thump. Thump. The footsteps were now in the clearing, drawing closer.

"Allie?! Are you here yet?" Stella called into the woods.

"Yes." Allie stepped out from behind the stump. "You ready?"

"Yes! I've got everything we could possibly need. Oh, and I checked my phone—tomorrow night is the next midnight full moon! We only have one day to find the portal before it disappears for another fourteen days!" Stella said, her voice tinged with excitement and a hint of nerves.

"Why did I expect that?" Allie sighed. "Okay, let's hike as far west as we can for now, then set up camp. Our parents will realize we're missing by morning, and they'll probably check the clearing first."

She tried to sound brave, but Stella was staring at the ground, her expression almost guilty. "Stella... what did you do?"

"Ehh, I left my parents a note," Stella admitted, looking up at Allie. "I told them what we think, what you can do, and not to call the police. But I didn't give them any details about where we'd be—just that we'd be gone for a few days and not to worry."

Allie could see the fear in Stella's eyes, and she knew how much this weighed on her.

"It's okay. Honestly, I did the same," Allie said with a smile. "I didn't want them calling the police when we're perfectly fine."

They both laughed, and for a brief moment, the weight of their adventure slipped away, leaving just the warmth of their friendship.

They had been walking all night, and Allie could feel her feet growing numb. "I think we've gone far enough," she said, sinking onto a low-hanging branch, relief washing over her.

"Wait, no! Not here. There's a clearing up ahead where we should camp," Stella said, glancing up from the map she had been studying all night. Her mom had taught her how to track their location using a paper map, a skill that proved invaluable as they hiked through the forest at five in the morning.

"Okay." Allie grunted but got to her feet and walked alongside Stella. She had to admit, Stella was right; a clearing lay just ahead. The moon bathed it in such bright light that Allie felt as if she were beneath the Star from the Christmas story.

They set up camp in silence, each lost in their own thoughts. *What if we don't find anything? What if this is all for nothing? I'll be Sephtis's slave! And what if we encounter him and don't even recognize him because we don't know what he looks like? Wait, we need to find out what he looks like... and I can shapeshift!*

"Stella, do you know what Sephtis looks like?" Allie asked.

"Umm, no. Nobody does. Remember?" Stella shot Allie a look that suggested she thought she was crazy.

"But we can find out," Allie urged, trying to get Stella to see the possibilities swirling in her mind.

"No, wait. Oh. Perfect!" Stella's eyes lit up as she looked at Allie and nodded. Allie stood in the center of their camp, her heart racing. *Turn into Sephtis.*

Allie opened her eyes, and it took Stella a moment to realize it was still her. Once she did, she quickly snapped a picture with her phone, wanting to capture the moment. Allie didn't want to stay in Sephtis's form any longer than necessary. She transformed back into herself and walked over to Stella to see the photo.

"Yep. Definitely Sephtis." He looked just like Allie had imagined when her dad described him in the story: a sludge-colored mane that flared like fire around his head, a grayish-black body, and red eyes that seemed to pierce right through her soul.

They decided to go to sleep soon after that. A few hours later, however, they were jolted awake by a thunderous roar.

"Roar!" A bear stood in their campsite, looming over them.

Stella let out a blood-curdling scream.

"Allie! We have to get out of here! Now!" Stella screamed as she dashed toward the trees.

"No! Don't move!" Allie shouted, but it was too late. The bear had spotted Stella and was charging straight toward her.

Stella had made it halfway across the clearing when the bear snatched her arm in its claws. Still screaming, she kicked at the bear's mouth as it lunged to take a bite.

Allie knew there was only one thing she could do. *Turn into a bear!*

Allie transformed into the massive creature and charged toward the bear pursuing Stella.

"Roar!" The bear snarled in anger, trying to tackle Allie to the ground. With a burst of determination, she darted to the far side of the clearing, ready to make one final stand.

Allie dashed in a circle, the bear close behind her. It was starting to lose its nerve. She leaped up to strike at the bear, again and again. Now both were on their hind legs, swiping at each other.

Allie crouched to kick the bear's legs out from under it, but as she did, its tooth snagged her arm as it tumbled down.

Ignoring the pain and the blood trickling from her arm, she lunged for the bear's neck. But just as she reached it, the bear finally surrendered and bolted away.

Out of breath, Allie collapsed to the ground. "Turn into me," she gasped. When Stella recognized that the bear that had just saved her was Allie, she rushed to her side. Stella's face was the last thing Allie saw before everything went black.

Stella looked down to see Allie's sleeve torn and stained with blood. A few drops from the bear's claws had landed on her neck, but they were so minor she hardly cared. Allie's arm, however, was another story. Stella was just relieved not to see any bone. Allie's sleeve was torn from shoulder to elbow.

Blood was running down her arm onto the ground and Stella's hands were also covered in it from getting the shirt out of the wound. Rushing to her first aid kit in her bag, Stella grabbed bandage wrap, disinfectant wipes, a needle, some thread, and paper towels. Carefully, she began to bandage Allie's arm...

Allie woke up on the bank of a river. As she sat up, she took in her surroundings: the flowing water to her right and a dense forest to her left.

She noticed a sharp pain in her left arm, and when she looked down, she saw it completely wrapped in bandages. For a brief moment, she forgot who she was and where she was—until Stella came running over to her.

"Oh, Allie! You're okay! I thought you were... well, never mind that. We have to go! And, um, sorry if you end up with a weird scar on your arm. My mom taught me how to stitch a few years ago, but I was never really that great at it."

"You've been out for five hours. It's noon. If we want to make it to the portal, we have to go now!" Stella jumped up and handed Allie her bag, suddenly very insistent.

"Stella, wait! Can you hold my bag?" Allie said, a spark of inspiration lighting up her eyes.

"Of course." Stella took it without hesitation.

"Get on my back in a second." Allie turned into a horse then turned to Stella and neighed.

Stella finally understood. "Oh, good idea! But is your arm okay? And where did the bandages go?" She looked down at Allie's front left leg.

Turn into myself. The bandages weren't there anymore, but a scar stretched from her shoulder to the back of her elbow.

"That's weird. It doesn't even hurt anymore," Allie said, bending and moving her leg.

"That's great! Now we don't have to worry about it."

Allie transformed back into a horse, and Stella hopped onto her back. Once settled, Allie reared up and began galloping west.

"I think we're lost," Stella said. Allie was still in her horse form, and they had been galloping for over four hours.

"Are we still going west?" Allie asked. Thankfully, Allie could still speak English, even as an animal.

Stella checked the compass. "Yes, but Allie, what if we've already passed it? It'll be midnight in a few hours."

"Oh, okay. Get off my back," Allie said. Stella hopped down, and Allie transformed into a giraffe. Now she could see over the treetops. "Alright, we'll wait until midnight, and hopefully I'll spot it. Then we can run to it and get through," Allie said.

"Were you talking? I can't hear you up there, Allie! Can you even hear me?" Stella shouted from below.

Turn into myself. Once she did, Allie repeated her words.

"Oh, okay. Sounds good to me. But how will we get there in time?" Stella always thought of every detail.

"Umm," Allie said, transforming into a cheetah. "Will this work?"

"Perfect!" Stella replied.

"See anything yet?" Stella called at eleven fifty-nine.

"No!" Allie replied. She had transformed into a giraffe a few minutes early, hoping to spot the portal right before midnight to give them more time to reach it. But things weren't turning out as planned.

The minute hand ticked forward on Stella's watch. Allie quickly scanned the area, and then, out of nowhere, she spotted the portal—a quick flash of light to her left. It was directly west.

"Get on!" Allie urged Stella as she transformed into a cheetah. They raced toward the light as fast as possible. When they rounded the corner, the sight took their breath away. Neither of them had seen anything like it before.

"What do you think it could be, Allie?" Stella asked quietly.

The light was coming from a keyhole in a door. It was a normal-sized wooden door, adorned with carvings that resembled constellations. There were no walls supporting the door—just a doorpost—and it seemed to lead only to the other side.

They approached the door cautiously, even though they knew time was slipping away. Stella reached out and grabbed the doorknob, but the moment she did, she was hurled backward, letting out a short, blood-curdling scream as if an invisible hand had thrown her.

"It burned me!" Stella exclaimed as Allie rushed over and knelt beside her. Sure enough, her hand was deep red and steaming, while the outer part, which had cooled, had turned a nasty black.

"How did it burn you?" Allie asked. She remembered there was a cooling pack in the first aid kit in her backpack, but as she started digging around, Stella stopped her.

"Allie, we don't have time for that! You try the door! You're the reason we're out here in the first place!"

Allie looked at her, stunned. "Are you mad at me?" she whispered.

"Try the door!" Stella insisted, her voice firm.

Without thinking, she dropped her backpack and ran to the door. As soon as she got close, it swung open, revealing a blanket of white where the forest had been. Allie walked around the door, but on the other side, she found only the back of a closed door. Confused, she noted that it was open from the front but closed from the back.

"What now, Allie?" Stella called as she came around the door.

"I guess we'll have to go through. We don't have any other choice."

Allie quickly stuffed everything into her backpack and helped Stella to her feet. Without shutting the door, they ran through, stepping into a blinding light. It felt as if they had entered an entirely new territory.

Then Allie heard police sirens. She and Stella peered through the door and saw red and blue lights flashing toward the forest. Suddenly, she heard her dad scream her name.

Then she heard her mother scream, "Allie, what's going on?"

"We have to go, now!" Stella whispered in her ear at the same moment.

Allie looked up at the moon, noticing it beginning to fall from its peak. They had no more than five seconds left.

"I'm sorry mom." Allie shouted back, "We will explain everything later." She grabbed the door knob and shut the door just as the moon fell from its peak.

The sound of the sirens faded away. Stella and Allie seemed to be standing on nothing. As soon as Allie shut the door, it vanished. They turned to take a step, but instead, they began to fall.

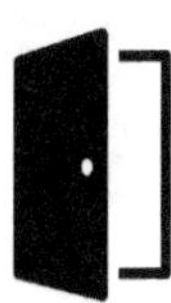

When she woke up, they were on what felt like solid ground, despite being surrounded by complete light.

"Ow." Came Stella's muffled voice. "You landed on my hand."

She suddenly realized that she had landed on top of Stella, quickly got up, and then helped Stella up.

"What now?" Allie asked, glancing around as Stella stood up.

"Allie, look—a door," Stella said in amazement. When Allie turned around, she saw that Stella was right. There was a door, the exact same size, color, and with the same carvings as the last one.

Stella peered through the keyhole. "I think this is it!" she exclaimed, turning to Allie and clapping. "Open it, Allie! Open it!"

She backed up to give Allie space. Taking a deep breath, Allie grasped the doorknob and turned it slowly. As soon as the door opened, they were sucked through like a vacuum, landing hard on the ground once again.

Chapter 8

"Y ou okay?" Allie asked Stella as her eyes came into focus. They seemed to be in the ruins of a castle. A wall loomed behind them, with the carved door they had just fallen through set into it. Allie lay on a patch of grass that had grown through the rock floor over the years.

"Yes. And Allie, look up." Allie glanced up to see Stella sitting on a rock, still cradling her hand. But Stella's gaze was fixed beyond Allie, staring at the world beyond the portal.

She slowly turned to face the world her friend was beholding. "Wow," she breathed.

It was nighttime, and the moon hung in the sky like a white candle in a dark room, illuminating the landscape before them.

In the distance, they could see the Snow Cap Peaks and the tips of the trees in Willows Wood just above the mist from Misty Meadows. Allie spotted the glimmer of the Lake of Memories. Sure enough, a shadow of the moon seemed to be painted on the mountains with black ink.

"This must be the Pertiaus Realm," Allie said.

"Okay, you need to rest your hand, and I have a first aid kit. I'll see what I can do. But first, we need to find a place to rest out of sight." Stella had her sketchbook out, drawing the Pertiaus Realm with her opposite hand, not looking up at Allie.

"Hold on. Let me finish."

"Stella..." Allie began, ready to list more reasons why they needed to move, but Stella interrupted her.

"Oh, alright. It's hard to draw with my left hand anyway," she said. Allie smiled as she helped Stella tuck her sketchbook back into her bag.

They began exploring the castle ruins. *I wonder if there's a nook somewhere,* Allie thought. But as they turned a corner, the scene shifted.

Built into the rocks was a quaint little cottage. Its roof and walls were made of stone, and since no smoke rose from the chimney, they started walking toward it.

This is a good place to rest and help Stella.

The room was dark, but by the light of the moon streaming through the window, Allie could just make out a lantern and some matches on a table. When she lit the lantern, the cottage came into view. The entire space was one room, and two of the four walls were lined with bookcases filled with books.

In the center of the room stood a table with four chairs, and on the far side was a bed.

"Aww, it's so cute," Stella said, walking over to one of the chairs to sit down. Allie, however, glanced at the books on the shelves and read one of the covers: "Creatures."

She walked over and picked up the book. It had a leather cover, and the script was fine and neatly written. The contents indicated that the book was divided into four parts, one for each region of that world. She flipped open to the section about the animals in the woods. The page displayed a picture of a cat, but instead of fur, it was covered in snake scales. Where a cat's nose should have been was a snake's mouth, and its fangs dripped with venom.

"Scaled Cat. Lives in the brush under Sneak Trap trees. Will eat meat or the leaves of a Frost Poppy plant. Beware of this animal."

Allie turned back a few pages to look at another creature.

"Cloud Dragon. This creature can blend into the mist and the various colors around it, often resembling soft clouds. However, it is as solid and real as you and me. Not all Cloud Dragons breathe fire; some can unleash different types of weather, such as water, lightning, or ice. They primarily eat meat and Cloud Puff plants. If you feed one a Sugar Puff plant, it will be your loyal pet forever."

At the bottom of the page, it read, "Little is known about Lightning Cloud Dragons."

This might come in handy, Allie thought as she showed Stella the book and then tucked it into her backpack. She walked over and pulled out a chair from the table to sit in, placing her bag on the table in front of her as she rummaged through her first aid kit.

Thankfully, there was a cold pack and some ace wrap in the kit. As Allie handed it to Stella, they heard footsteps approaching outside. Suddenly, the door squeaked open behind them. Allie felt a gasp escape her lips, followed by the sound of a sword sliding from its sheath, sending a shiver down her spine.

"Freeze! Stand up and turn around!"

With their backs to the door, they couldn't see who had spoken. Instead, they both nodded and then turned around.

In the doorway stood a girl about their height. Her skin was tanned from spending long hours in the sun, and her dark brown hair was pulled back into a messy bun. She wore jean shorts and a fitted crop top, with a worn black leather jacket draped over her shirt. Her black combat boots were tied in tight bows, and a sword sheath hung at her waist, the sword gripped in her hands like a baseball bat, ready to swing.

"Who are you, and what do you think you're doing in my house?" she demanded, shutting the door behind her while keeping the sword raised.

Silence.

"ANSWER ME! And don't even think about using magic against me in my own home."

"Magic? What do you mean by magic..." Stella began, but Allie interrupted, sensing the tension in her friends voice.

"Yeah, we don't know what you're talking about. We don't have any magic."

"LIARS!" The girl put the tip of her sword on Allie's neck. She heard Stella gasp right behind her, and Allie could swear everyone could hear her heart pounding.

"Um, my name is Stella, and this is my friend Allie. We've come to find Sephtis. Can we start over?"

And put the sword down?! Allie added silently in her head.

"Yeah, we didn't know this house was occupied. Sorry," Allie said, irritation creeping into her tone.

"Sephtis? THE Sephtis?" the girl repeated, lowering her sword slightly, only to quickly raise it again. "How do I know I can trust you?"

"You can trust us. We crossed over the portal just a few minutes ago, and I promise we mean no harm," Stella said, sounding strikingly like her mother.

The girl looked shocked. "You came through the portal?"

"Yes," they both replied in unison.

"Okay, sit down. It seems we need to talk." She bolted the door and sheathed her sword.

The girl started asking Stella and Allie questions about how they found the portal and why they needed to find Sephtis. She seemed genuinely interested in their connection to him. As the conversation continued, Allie found herself growing increasingly irritated with Stella.

Allie thought to herself, *How could Stella be so open with someone who had just put a sword to her best friend's throat?* As her irritation grew, Stella interrupted the girl and asked:

"What is your name?" It was just like Stella to ask that question first.

"And what are you doing on this side of the portal?" Allie added, eager to gather as much important information as possible so they could figure out a way to leave.

"My name is Amber, and I ended up here a long time ago. I was six at the time."

"How old are you now?" Stella asked.

"Fourteen, I think," Amber replied, gazing into the distance, lost in thought.

"So how did you end up here?" Allie pressed, wanting to clarify. Amber still hadn't answered her question.

With a sigh, Amber looked back at them, deep reflection in her eyes, and began to share her story.

"My dad was one of the builders in the legend. I'm sure you know that story since you know about Sephtis. He and a few other men decided to follow Sephtis through the portal. My mom went too, bringing me along. When Sephtis found out there were humans in this world, he was furious and cast a spell over the portal."

"The spell was meant to pull only non-magical beings to the other world. All the workers and my parents were forced out, but for some reason, the portal wouldn't let me through, no matter how many times I tried. In the end, he banished me to an 'In Between World' for a hundred years."

"Eight years ago, he finally let me out. I was still the same age, and it felt like just a second to me. I pleaded with Sephtis to let me go, but he only ever replied, 'When my spell over mankind is complete, you may pass through the portal.'"

"So I came here, built a home, and began learning how to defend myself. I studied every plant and animal, even figuring out how to communicate with some of the creatures. I documented all the information I gathered, creating the books that fill this place."

For the first time since the girls had entered it, silence fell over the cottage.

"That's..." Stella began, but Allie, still irritated with her, interrupted with what she thought was a more pressing statement.

"So wait, you wrote all these books?" Allie asked, considering that each one was handwritten and must have taken a lot of time and patience.

"Yep. Every single one," Amber replied.

Silence fell again as Stella and Allie replayed Amber's story in their minds. *If I can find Sephtis, Amber will be free to leave.* Allie glanced at Stella, giving a slight nod toward Amber. As best friends, they shared an immediate understanding of each other's thoughts. Stella responded with a nod.

"Amber, I left out a part of my story. I didn't tell you everything about why I came to find Sephtis," Allie said.

"What did you leave out?" Amber asked, her curiosity piqued. Allie chose her words carefully, noticing that Amber had placed a hand on the hilt of her sword without drawing it.

Deep breath. "Just... come outside."

Allie stood up, and Amber followed, curiosity evident in her eyes, though she never took her hand off her sword.

"Okay, don't scream. Just name an animal," Allie said, standing on a flat rock facing the cottage. "Do you remember any from the other world?"

"Oh, I remember this creature called a falcon, I think..."

Turn into a falcon. Allie felt herself transform mid-sentence and took off, avoiding eye contact with Amber.

She only stayed up there for a minute. When she landed, she thought, *Turn into me.* Not wanting to make eye contact just yet, she walked slowly into the cottage, leaving Amber behind.

"How'd it go?" Stella asked.

"Don't know yet. We're about to find out." Allie replied just as Amber walked into the cottage.

Amber stared at Allie, her mouth agape. Slowly, she found her voice. "First of all, you lied to me. You do have magic."

Allie threw her arms in the air, frustrated that this was beside the point.

"And second," Amber continued, ignoring Allie entirely.

"'The child will have abilities beyond your wildest imaginations,'" she recited from the story. "You're the kid from the tale!" Amber exclaimed, her excitement palpable. "Wait, how old are you?"

"That's why we're here. Allie's fourteenth birthday is in five days, and we don't know anything about this world. I thought we could help each other," Stella explained.

Allie quickly glanced at Stella. "We did?"

"Yes, we did. You have to admit, we need her help," Stella replied firmly.

Amber had tuned out the girls' conversation, lost in her own thoughts. When the cottage fell silent, she turned to them.

"Well, first, do you know how to find Sephtis?" Amber asked.

"Yes. My friend and I did a lot of research before coming," Allie said. Realizing that Stella was right, she felt a wave of guilt for having gotten mad at her.

"This all started when I felt something strange at school..."

47

Chapter 9

By candlelight, Stella and Allie took turns recounting the events of the past two days, beginning with their time at school. They shared their notes and the map they had acquired, eager to provide Amber with every detail.

"So we need to reach Snow Cap Peaks?" Amber asked when they finished.

"Yes! And what's a Sneak Trap Tree?" Allie replied, pulling the 'Creatures' book from her backpack and flipping to the page about the 'Scaled Cat.'

"It's a tree with branches that can move on their own. Get too close, and they'll grab you in the blink of an eye." Amber stood up, retrieved a 'Plants' book, and flipped to a page. She held the book out for Stella and Allie to see. "See? This book is just as important as the animal one."

"Oh, thank you! Do you think you could help us find Sephtis?" Stella asked, voicing Allie's question. They both hoped she would join them; having someone familiar with this world—and armed with a sword—would be a great advantage.

"Yes! Once we find Sephtis, I can finally go through the portal." Amber's smile had been growing ever since she discovered a way to get home.

"Okay, great! We can leave in the morning," Allie said, eager to turn words into action.

The next morning, Stella declared her hand felt better, so they set out toward the Misty Meadows. Amber insisted that both Stella and Allie take swords, even though they had no idea how to use them. Amber had warned them that if they got separated, they would need the swords to defend against some of the creatures in that world. As they made their way toward the meadows, she gave them a quick overview of the plants and animals they might encounter.

"The most important thing is to stay away from the mist balls. They're clumps of mist that shoot into the sky and fall back down every hour. If one touches you, you'll be frozen for life. Also, don't eat any berries unless I've approved them—there are many poisonous kinds out there. Got it?" Amber's eyes sparkled with excitement at the thought of going on an adventure with others.

"Sure! So, what plants can we eat?" Stella asked. Allie had insisted on keeping the bandage around her hand, even though Stella assured her she was fine. But Allie could see the pain lingering in Stella's eyes.

"The only plant you can eat is a Cloud Puff plant. They are not hard to find, but very hard to get. Cloud Dragons love that plant and spend their whole life protecting them. If you find one you must trade the dragon for one."

"What can you trade it for?" Allie asked.

"Well, Cloud Dragons love their shinies," Amber said, pulling a few bright crystals from her pocket. She winked at Allie. "Just in case."

"So, how do you find a Cloud Puff plant?" Stella asked.

"You'll see a pile of gold. The plant is large enough for the dragons to sleep on, so they keep all their treasure underneath it," Amber explained.

"Ooh, that sounds pretty," Stella said, daydreaming.

"Didn't the book say the dragon will become your loyal pet?" Allie asked, climbing over a rock.

"Yes, but only if you feed it a Sugar Puff plant, which grows at the bottom of the Twin River," Amber replied.

"Twin River?" Stella asked.

"Yes, the Twin River has a 'twin' running parallel to it a mile away, called the Parallel River," Amber said with a chuckle.

"Don't you think we should get some of that to feed a dragon? We could ride it over the meadows!" Stella suggested.

"It *would* make the trip faster," Allie said. "but, we don't have to do that. I could turn into a dragon myself, right?" She smiled.

Amber replied, "Yes, you can turn into a dragon. However, only one of us could ride you." Allie's smile faded. "So we do need to find one, but the Twin River is really deep..." Amber paused, stopping in her tracks. She looked around quickly and pulled out her sword. "Wait, I hear something."

Stella and Allie froze instantly.

Amber was right; the bushes to their left were rustling. Just as Allie considered the possibilities, a Scaled Cat leaped out, charging straight at Stella.

"Why is it always me?" Stella cried as the cat charged at her.

Before Allie could react with her own sword, Amber brought hers down on the cat, stopping it midair. When Allie glanced down, she saw the life had left the cat's eyes.

"I thought Scaled Cats lived in Willows Wood," Allie said, horrified as she stared at the lifeless body on the ground. She quickly went over to help Stella before Amber could respond.

"You okay?" she asked when she reached Stella.

"Yeah," Stella replied, looking at Amber who was cleaning her sword. "Thank you for saving me."

"Anytime. I'm glad you're okay. But to answer your question, Allie, yes, they do live in Willows Wood. It must be migration season. If that's the case, we need those dragons," Amber said, glancing around before she sheathed her sword.

"Okay, so we need to go to Twin River then?" Stella said, standing up.

A deep growl answered her question.

"Wind Lions!" Amber exclaimed.

"They don't happen to be herbivores, do they?" Allie asked, already knowing the answer.

"No. They're 100% meat-eaters! They must have smelled the cat." Amber already had her sword in hand again. "We need to get to the river—now!" She began running east, away from the deafening roars that were quickly closing in on the trio.

Allie and Stella followed her, running harder and faster, but they could still hear the lions clearly pursuing them instead of the cat. Suddenly, a new sound emerged—the magnificent rush of water. Amber slowed her pace to run alongside Stella and Allie.

"When we get to the river, jump. There's nothing that could hurt you beneath the surface," Amber said. They nodded in agreement.

Moments later, they stood before the wide, rushing river. Amber kept running and leaped in, but Allie and Stella hesitated. They turned around to see the Wind Lions—gray, lion-shaped creatures—emerging from the tree line.

"Come on!" Allie shouted, grabbing Stella's arm and jumping into the river. They were immediately swept downstream by the strong current toward Amber.

"Amber! Help Stella get to the other side! I'll get the Sugar Puff plant!" Allie yelled.

"No, Allie! It's too deep!" Stella cried.

Turn into a fish! Allie thought, turning to them. "Trust me!"

Finally, Amber nodded, and Allie dove beneath the surface.

Chapter 10

The water was cool and smooth. As Allie swam deeper, the current grew weaker. Soon, she reached a depth where the water was as still as a pond. She dove to the bottom to search for the plant they needed.

She searched for a while, and after having no luck, started to wish she had asked Amber what the plants looked like. Allie swam to a part of the riverbed that appeared to be covered in cotton candy. *That can't be right,* she thought. As she leaned in for a closer look, she realized they were, in fact, plants.

Turn into a mermaid, she thought. Allie gathered what looked like enough for three dragons and swam back to the surface. She kicked her tail, propelling herself upward, and leaped above the water. Mid-air, she transformed into an eagle, gliding down to her friends on the riverbank before shifting back to her human form.

"I got it!" She said holding it up as she caught her breath.

"Oh good." Amber said plainly.

Stella looked at Amber. "Amber, Allie just went to the bottom of this river while we were resting on the shore. The least you could do is offer some gratitude." Stella grumbled.

Amber shook her head, as if clearing her thoughts. "Oh right. I'm sorry, Allie. I was just trying to figure out what to do next." She moved over to help Allie up.

"It's okay," Allie replied with a grunt as she stood and looked around.

"So, this is Misty Meadows?"

"Yep. We're in Misty Meadows. The river marks the border. All we have to do now is find three dragons," Amber said sarcastically. "Easy enough."

They all shared a small laugh before continuing deeper into Misty Meadows. Soon, they were engulfed in mist. For Allie, it felt like a rainforest, filled with mist and flowers—just without the rain.

Stella pointed to a golden light on their right and started running. "Look! I think I found one." She called over her shoulder while still running.

Amber and Allie looked at each other and then took off after her.

When they caught up to Stella, she stood before a massive, sleeping dragon. It resembled a gigantic lizard with wings, just as Allie had imagined.

"Quick, give me some of that Sugar Puff," Stella whispered.

"No, Stella! You'll be eaten!" Allie whispered, not wanting to witness her friend get pulverized.

"She's fine," Amber assured her. But Allie still felt uneasy. Reluctantly, she handed some of the Sugar Puff to Stella.

Stella then walked right up to the dragon and put her hand on its nose. "Wake up, I brought you some Sugar Puffs." Then she held the plant close to its nose so the dragon could smell it.

It felt like an eternity before the dragon lifted its head and looked at Stella, staring intently for what seemed like ages. Amber and Allie both screamed when the dragon suddenly leaped down between them and Stella, its face so close that Allie could see the white in its eyes.

"Don't come close to this human."

Allie looked around, wondering who had spoken. "Who's talking to me?"

"Can you understand me?"

The voice flowed like a calm river—unlike anything she had heard before. Allie stared at the dragon in amazement. "Is it you?"

"If you're asking if I'm the one speaking to you, then yes. It has been so long since anyone has heard my voice. Because you can understand me, I will allow you to explain yourself. So I'll ask again: why do you approach

this human?" The dragon's calming voice held a slight growl beneath it.

"Um, she's my best friend, and we wanted to ask if you would help us find Sephtis. We heard that if you give a Cloud Dragon some Sugar Puff Plants, they'll be your loyal friend forever. Is that true?" Allie asked the dragon.

"Allie, who are you talking to?" Amber asked, sounding doubtful, but Allie ignored her. The dragon spoke again.

"Yes, that is true. I will help you. I cannot personally fly you to Sephtis, as I am getting too old. However, I will introduce you to three young dragons who will become your friends if you offer them some Sugar Puff."

"Oh, thank you so much! Um, what is your name?" Allie asked the dragon, knowing Stella would want to know.

"Oh yes, I'm so sorry! I am Queen Mistyfoot of all the Cloud Dragons. Now I will summon some of the younger dragons." The Queen lifted her head and began to call three other dragons with a beautiful song.

"Umm, Allie, what's going on?" Amber asked.

"She was talking to me. This is Queen Mistyfoot of the Cloud Dragons. She's calling three dragons to help us," Allie said excitedly.

"Really? That's amazing! I wonder why we can't talk to the dragons," Amber stated, looking up at the Queen.

"I was wondering that too. But right now, we should find Stella and let her know we weren't eaten." They laughed as they ran to locate her.

"Are you guys okay?" Stella asked, emerging from behind the dragon. They nearly crashed into her.

"Yes, we're okay! Allie can talk to the dragon! Apparently, she's Queen Mistyfoot of the Cloud Dragons and is calling three of them to help us. Isn't that great?" Amber exclaimed.

"Wait. Slow down. Allie can talk to dragons?" Stella asked, turning to her. Before Allie could respond, Mistyfoot lowered her head and turned to her.

"They are coming. These dragons will be very loyal to you for the rest of your life."

"Thank you, Mistyfoot. Could you speak out loud so my friends can hear you too?" She wanted everyone to be able to talk to their dragons as well.

Allie could tell Mistyfoot was considering it. *"Due to dragon tradition, I'm only allowed to speak to other dragons or those who can hear me in their minds. But the younger dragons can talk freely, and I'll instruct them to do so."*

"Thank you." Just as Allie spoke, three magnificent dragons landed just a few feet from the Queen, each with unique colors and scales.

While the Queen shimmered in golden hues with light pink wings and white legs, the other dragons displayed brighter, bolder colors. The one closest to her was a dark red dragon adorned with an orange stripe down his belly. The next one was bright green with purple belly and horns. And the last one was silver with golden horns and spikes down her back.

The Queen gazed at them and began to speak, but this time, Allie couldn't hear her words. Mistyfoot then turned to Allie and nodded. With a few gentle flaps of her wings, she gracefully landed on her flower.

"Oh, this is so exciting! I'm finally going to be paired with a human!" exclaimed the green dragon, startling the others.

"Chill out, Seaspring. You're going to scare them," replied the red dragon, and he was right—their shocked expressions said it all.

"Bloodwing, Seaspring, calm down," the silver dragon interjected, as Seaspring rattled her wings in excitement.

"Ugh, Silverspark, chill! If Queen Mistyfoot called us, then we're the right dragons for the job," Seaspring huffed. "Now be quiet. I think they have Sugar Puffs." With that, the other two dragons fell silent.

"Um... yes, we have Sugar Puffs," Allie said. She slowly turned to Amber and Stella, breaking off two pieces of the plant and handing them over. "Go pick your dragon. And good luck," she whispered before turning back around.

They stood in a line before the dragons. Amber approached Bloodwing, offering him the plant. He grunted and lowered his head, allowing her to climb onto his back.

"What is your name, brave one?" he asked.

"My name is Amber," she replied, smiling at Stella and Allie.

"Hello, Amber. I'm Bloodwing. As Dragon Tradition dictates, I will be your loyal friend forever," he said.

Allie and Stella exchanged glances. Allie approached the silver dragon, Silverspark, eager since they had landed to make her her dragon. Just then, Stella walked toward Seaspring. Allie offered Silverspark her Sugar Puff plant and was permitted to climb onto her back. Like Bloodwing, she asked her name.

"What is your name, young one?"

"Allie."

"Nice to meet you, Allie. I'm Silverspark. As Dragon Tradition dictates, I will be your loyal friend forever," she said, echoing Bloodwing's words.

Allie heard Seaspring speaking to Stella.

"Greetings, Stella. I'm Seaspring. As Dragon Tradition dictates, I will be your loyal friend forever," she said.

Allie glanced at Amber and Stella; both were grinning, and so was she.

"So, where are we headed?" Seaspring asked after everyone had acquainted themselves with their dragons.

Amber and Stella glanced at Allie, who understood their unspoken question. She nodded, signaling that it was okay to share their purpose with the dragons.

"We need to find Sephtis," Amber said. She leaned over and whispered something into Bloodwing's ear.

"What are you talking about? No secrets between the best of friends! We can tell each other anything, right, Stella?" Seaspring asked, noticing Amber whispering to Bloodwing. Allie could already tell Seaspring was the talkative one in the group—a perfect match for Stella.

When Seaspring said that, Silverspark lowered her head slightly in front of Allie. Just as Allie was about to ask if she was okay, Amber responded to Seaspring.

"Oh, it's nothing. I was just telling Bloodwing what Allie can do," Amber said, shrugging it off as if it were no big deal. Apparently, Silverspark didn't take it so well and jumped slightly.

"Wait! Allie has a power and she didn't tell me?" Silverspark gasped, craning her neck to look at her. "We're supposed to share everything!" Allie noticed a glimmer behind Silverspark's eyes but managed to laugh through her confusion. "Silverspark, I've only been on your back for about thirty seconds, and you've been doing all the talking! There was no time to tell you!"

"Okay, well you can tell me now," Silverspark said, looking at her impatiently. At the same time, Queen Mistyfoot shifted in her flower, reminding everyone to be quiet.

"I'll tell you, Silverspark. But first, we need to find a place where we won't upset the Queen," she whispered.

"Good idea! Ooo! Our first ride with humans!" Seaspring squealed, launching into the air without warning Stella. Stella let out a startled scream but quickly grabbed hold of Seaspring's neck.

Bloodwing and Amber took off right behind them.

"Hey, wait for us!" Silverspark called, leaping into the air after them.

Although Allie was the only one of the three girls who had flown before, the thrill of riding on a dragon was still exhilarating. She and Silverspark quickly caught up to Seaspring and Bloodwing.

"So, where do you want to go?" Amber asked.

"This way!" Bloodwing replied mischievously, soaring straight up. Seaspring gasped and shot after him.

"What do you think? Should we follow?" Silverspark asked Allie.

"Yes!" Allie replied, eager to see what had excited Bloodwing. Besides, they couldn't get separated; their journeys were now intertwined.

As soon as Seaspring and Silverspark caught up to Bloodwing, he glanced back over his shoulder and dove straight down toward the ground.

Silverspark huffed. "We just came from there!" she shouted after Bloodwing, but he ignored her.

"Last one to the Dragon Heart is a rotten dragon egg!" Bloodwing called back, laughter in his voice.

"Come on, Silverspark! It looks like fun!" Seaspring exclaimed, looping in the sky before diving down backward.

Allie noticed that while Stella was enjoying herself, there was also a hint of fear and concern in her eyes. She was quickly learning that Seaspring loved to take chances.

"Come on, Silverspark! I don't want to lose!" Allie laughed at how cautious she was being. She figured they could have a little fun before embarking on their dangerous journey.

"You're right. We're going to win this!" she said, then dipped her nose and tucked her wings, diving straight down through the clouds.

Riding on Silverspark was unlike anything Allie had ever experienced. Soaring up and down on invisible waves in the sky and weaving through loops in the clouds was a sensation she would not soon forget.

As they neared the ground, they spotted a massive rock formation featuring a large carving of a dragon. The entrance to a cave was located where its heart would be.

Bloodwing led the way through the cave entrance, followed closely by Silverspark. Seaspring trailed in last, clearly upset about being the "rotten egg." Deeper into the tunnel, they entered a spacious chamber that seemed to be the main room.

All around the cavern, young dragons were gathered. On the far side, five or six targets were painted on rocks, and young Cloud Dragons took turns practicing their aim, trying to blast them with fire, water, or ice.

On the other end of the room, rocks were arranged in circles where groups of dragons sat, talking and laughing. The ceiling soared so high that they could barely see the top, but Allie noticed ropes and hoops hanging down, creating a sort of ropes course for the dragons. Each took turns flying through it.

"What is this place?" Allie asked Silverspark.

"This is the Dragon Heart. It's a place where all dragons can come to hang out, practice, and have fun.

"That's so cool." Allie looked back at Stella, who was sitting on Seaspring behind her. "It's like a dragon hangout!"

"Amazing!" Stella exclaimed.

Bloodwing led them into a hallway on the opposite side of the chamber, lined with doors—some open and some closed. Laughter came from behind the closed doors, while the open ones revealed empty rooms. He guided them to the last open door in the hallway.

Inside, huge petals from Cloud Puff plants were shaped like chairs, forming a circle in the cozy room.

Amber dismounted from Bloodwing and settled into a chair.

"This is so cool, Bloodwing! Now we can talk without bothering anyone," Amber exclaimed.

"Yes, and now everyone take a seat. I want to hear Allie's power," Silverspark said after closing the door.

Once everyone had settled into their seats, Allie began her story. She had asked Stella and Amber not to mention her power yet, so they took turns sharing bits of the story leading up to the moment they met the dragons.

"So you've lived here almost your whole life?" Bloodwing asked Amber.

"Sephtis's enchantment is over you?" Silverspark asked Allie.

"You went with Allie on this dangerous mission just because she's your best friend?" Seaspring questioned Stella.

Amber, Stella, and Allie exchanged glances with each other and then with their dragons.

"Yes," they all replied simultaneously.

"Wow, okay, now, um... Allie. What... is... your... power...?" Silverspark asked, clearly impatient.

Allie laughed. "Okay, okay," she said, then leaned toward Stella and whispered, "Yell out a few animals from our world." Allie stood up in the center of the circle of chairs.

Looking at the dragons, Allie asked, "Are you ready?"

"Yes," they replied.

Allie gave Stella a thumbs up, and immediately Stella began calling out types of animals so quickly that Allie actually missed a few. When they finished, the dragons were gawking at Allie.

"That is so cool, Allie! You can shapeshift!" Silverspark squealed.

"Well, thank you," Allie replied.

"Oh! And I forgot to tell all of you what I meant by magic in the cottage," Amber added.

"Yes, I meant to ask about that," Stella said, sitting up quickly with curiosity.

"So, normally people aren't as strong as I am. I've discovered that some people have magic since being in this place. That's what I meant. I don't know where it came from, but I only had it when I entered this realm."

"That makes more sense. I'd love to discuss this more, but we need to get going if we want to find Sephtis before my birthday," Allie said, only half listening to what Amber had said.

"Okay, good thinking. But I sense a storm brewing—a bad one. We'll stay dry and safe if we make it to the Walk," Seaspring replied.

"What's the Walk?" Stella asked.

Amber stood up. "It's a part of Willows Wood where the trees are so thick they create a 'ceiling,' forcing you to walk. That ceiling will keep the water away if there's a bad storm, and around here, they're usually like hurricanes. So we need to hurry!" she said, hopping onto Bloodwing's back.

Chapter 11

It had only been a few minutes since they left Misty Meadows when the sky began to rumble. They flew over the treetops between Misty Meadows and Willows Wood, heading for the Walk, but they weren't sure if they would reach it before the rain started.

"I don't think we're going to make it to the Walk," Seaspring said nervously, glancing up at the sky.

"Don't worry, I'm here," Bloodwing puffed out his chest as if he could stop the storm, while Silverspark rolled her eyes. "Besides, there hasn't been any lightning yet."

Not a second after Bloodwing said that, lightning flashed across the sky.

"You were saying?" Allie remarked as she, Silverspark, Seaspring, and Stella sped past him, trying to pick up the pace.

A little later, it started to rain.

"Can you see anything?" Allie heard Amber yell from the back of Bloodwing. Although she wasn't sure who Amber was addressing, she replied anyway.

"No, I can't even see my hand in front of my face."

"How are we going to find the Walk in this weather?" Allie called out. *What if we've already passed it?* she thought.

There was a long moment of silence among the group, but the storm was anything but quiet. It growled at them from every direction, and the rain fell so hard that each drop felt like a needle.

"I have an idea. Y'all stay here!" Silverspark hollered, shooting up toward the clouds and lightning so quickly that Allie screamed.

"Silverspark! What are you doing? We're going to get hit by lightning!" she yelled, terrified.

"Exactly why I'm here," Silverspark replied.

Allie was certain she hadn't heard her correctly.

Suddenly, flashes of lightning streaked down around them in a circle.

But instead of flashing quickly and disappearing, the lights remained, surrounding them. Then Allie realized Silverspark was flying straight toward the lightning. Finally, one struck her square in the chest.

"Silverspark!" Allie screamed in terror.

"Yes!" Allie heard Silverspark cry, but then her whole body went cold, and they began to fall. Allie shut her eyes, lying flat on Silverspark's back, bracing for impact. When she opened her eyes, she heard their friends yelling her name as they passed by. Glancing down, she noticed a soft glow in Silverspark's chest—it looked like a heartbeat.

What? Allie thought.

Silverspark's heart glowed softly, growing brighter and brighter. Then, as if it were spreading through her veins, the glow coursed through Allie's body.

Allie felt Silverspark warm up and saw her eyes open. Silverspark then spread her brightly glowing wings, catching the air and soaring up to the others.

"Silverspark, how are you glowing?" Bloodwing asked.

"And how are y'all alive?!?" Amber exclaimed. "I've never heard of anything like this, especially with the lightning around here."

Stella and Seaspring nodded in agreement. Allie felt just as clueless as they were.

"I'm a Lightning Cloud Dragon. It's what we do." Then, instead of breathing fire, she opened her mouth and shot a string of electricity into the sky.

"Silverspark, that's amazing!" Allie exclaimed.

"And now, I can help light the way so we can find the Walk," Silverspark said. Allie finally understood why they had to be struck by lightning.

"Yeah, but I thought Lightning Cloud Dragons were extinct," Amber pondered aloud.

"Well, THIS Cloud Dragon would like to get out of the rain. Come on!" Seaspring said, taking off into the sky.

Within minutes of flying, they reached the Walk. Silverspark, Seaspring, and Bloodwing landed near a line of tall pine trees, and Silverspark's glow faded. Just as Amber had described, the branches were woven together, forming the "ceiling" of the Walk. Beyond that, all Allie could see was mist and darkness.

"I'm not so sure about this," Allie heard Stella whisper.

"Welcome to the Walk," Amber began in a voice reminiscent of a horror movie narrator. "Beyond this point, you enter the unknown. Unknown creatures and unknown dangers await you in this forest."

Everyone felt a bit hesitant.

"Okay, let's get out of this rain," Allie said.

As they slowly entered the Walk, the rain ceased, replaced by mist and darkness. Silverspark lost sight of Bloodwing and Seaspring, and it was only the sound of their voices that kept them from getting lost.

"Silverspark, light up!" Allie whispered urgently.

"I can't right now. I need time to recharge," Silverspark replied quietly.

"Recharge? Now?" Allie's voice grew louder.

"It's something Lightning Cloud Dragons have to do. We need lightning to glow. I should be fine in a few minutes."

Allie remembered reading a book in her youth about a place just like the Walk, inhabited only by the most dangerous creatures, masters of disguise. If you encountered those creatures, you would only live on in people's memories. As Allie recalled that story, she became increasingly attuned to the sounds of the forest. Just as she felt she might lose her mind, Bloodwing announced that they had reached a cave.

"We can't go any further tonight. Follow my voice to enter the cave. Be careful! There's a low branch right before the entrance. Silverspark, can you light up and gather some firewood? Amber and Allie, please clear the floor. Stella and Seaspring, head to the river for water and food for tonight. Thanks," Bloodwing instructed.

"Okay, Sir Bloodwing. But what are you going to do? Hang around here and sleep?" Seaspring snorted in disgust. It was clear she was upset that Bloodwing would send the girls into the dangerous woods while he stayed safely in the cave.

"What! No! I'm staying here to help Amber and Allie and protect them from the... the... I don't know. But I'll protect them from something!" Bloodwing snorted indignantly.

"Uh-huh. Come on, Stella, let's go get the water," Seaspring said with a yawn.

"Silverspark, are you okay?" Allie asked her.

"Yeah, I should be fine now," Silverspark replied, starting to glow.

Once Seaspring, Stella, and Silverspark left for the supplies, Bloodwing began to pace.

"Okay, Bloodwing. Why are you doing that?" Amber asked, her tone suggesting she suspected he was up to something.

Bloodwing let out a small huff and sat down. "I just realized I shouldn't have sent them out in this weather, and I'm worried about Sea—I mean, all of them," he said, a slight flush creeping into his cheeks.

"It's okay, Bloodwing," Amber began, trying not to laugh. "We know you have a little crush on Sea—"

"I do not!" Bloodwing interrupted, jumping back up, his embarrassment evident.

"You're very bad at lying," Amber said, enjoying the chance to tease her dragon. "Where was I? Oh yes, you don't want her to get hurt. But we care about Stella and Silverspark as well. You might be right that sending them out there wasn't the best idea, but it's done now. We can't dwell on what we could've done. Instead, let's focus on getting this place ready for their return."

Once she finished her speech, they all continued working in the cave. It was a while before anyone spoke.

"Are either of you going to say anything to Seaspring?" Bloodwing asked the girls, unsure how they would react to his admission of liking her.

Allie laughed. "No, Bloodwing. If you don't want us to, we won't mention anything," she said.

"Good," Bloodwing replied, giving a satisfied nod.

Once that was settled, they resumed cleaning the cave. In the silence, Allie realized for the first time that Amber was showing a very different side of her from when they had first met. Before long, Seaspring, Stella, and Silverspark returned with water, food, and firewood. Amber, the only one who knew how to set up the wood for the campfire, had a great time trying to teach them.

No one seemed awake enough to learn how to build a fire, so Amber ended up doing it herself. While she worked on the wood, Stella and Allie set up tents on the other side of the cave for the girls to sleep in. Once the wood was ready, Bloodwing ignited it into a mighty blaze.

"Be careful. Make sure it doesn't get too toasty in here," Seaspring said, sitting down next to Allie, who had just joined her at the fire after finishing the tent with Stella. "That's the nice way of saying, 'Don't burn us, Bloodwing,'" she whispered to Allie, her voice dripping with disgust.

It was almost as if Seaspring had put up an emotional wall toward Bloodwing during their time in the woods.

"Don't worry, I know how to make a nice fire. Calm yourself," Bloodwing said.

"Excuse me!" Seaspring exclaimed, jumping up and spreading her wings as if ready to confront a massive dragon like Bloodwing.

"No, Seaspring, we're not going to fight," Stella said, stroking Seaspring's back. "If the fire gets out of control, you can always put it out with your water power."

"Fine. If you say so, it's time to sleep anyway. Good night *girls*," Seaspring said, settling into the far nook of the cave.

"She didn't say goodnight to me," Bloodwing remarked, dropping his head as he slowly walked to the other end of the cave.

Amber and Stella exchanged a glance before both rushing to their dragons, leaving Silverspark and Allie by themselves near the fire.

"What's going on between Bloodwing and Seaspring?" Allie asked Silverspark.

"I don't know. They've always been really good friends," Silverspark replied.

They sat in silence for a little longer, lost in their thoughts.

"Well, good night, I guess," Allie said, using Silverspark's leg as a pillow.

"Night, Allie."

Soon, everyone fell asleep with their own dragon, the tents forgotten.

Chapter 12

Once they all awakened, Allie and Stella took down the tents and stowed them in their backpacks. Seaspring walked over and drenched the fire, ensuring it was completely out. Satisfied, Stella, Amber, and Allie mounted their dragons, and they continued their trek toward Snow Cape Peaks.

The only time Allie had seen the Walk was the night before during the storm. Though it was still raining, it wasn't a lightning storm, which was a relief. It was also much brighter than the previous night, allowing her to finally see the trees surrounding them.

Aside from the pitter-patter of rain on the trees, it was silent—so silent it felt almost eerie. No birds sang in the branches, and no squirrels played on the trunks. It was as if the forest was devoid of life.

"Okay, follow me. Amber and I talked last night, and I know how to get us out of here," Bloodwing said.

"Yes, let's follow Bloodwing. I trust him, and I know he knows the way," Seaspring added.

They all turned around.

"Seaspring, I thought you were mad at Bloodwing last night?" Silverspark and Stella asked in unison.

"Haha! Why would I be mad at one of my best friends? Good one, guys. Okay, let's go," she said with a smile, then started following Bloodwing, who was already leaving the clearing.

"That was weird," Allie said to Silverspark.

"Yeah, but we need to keep moving. We can think about it later," Silverspark replied.

Then Allie noticed they were the only ones left in the clearing in front of the cave. Everyone else had walked down a path, and Silverspark started to follow. After a little while, they turned a corner and spotted Amber standing there with a book in her hand. She walked up to them and handed Allie the book.

"Read this. Page 87, about the plants," Amber instructed before running to Bloodwing and hopping on his back. Allie tried to open the book, but quickly realized it was locked, just like the other one. The key was in her backpack....

"Silverspark! Go back to the cave right now!" Allie exclaimed. She had forgotten her backpack and couldn't believe she had been so careless.

Silverspark quickly turned around and dashed back to the cave, retracing the path they had just taken. Allie hurried inside and grabbed her backpack.

"Maybe we can follow the path back a little," Allie suggested, scanning the surroundings for any sign of the others. "They can't be too far ahead."

Silverspark shook her head, her eyes dull with sadness.

"Are you serious? We just came from there! How can we not know where to go?" Allie scoffed.

"Well, Bloodwing mentioned there was a fork in the path a few feet from where we left, but he didn't say which way they were going."

"Wait! Stella and I brought our phones. I can call her!" Allie exclaimed, eagerly digging into her backpack.

"What's a phone?" Silverspark asked.

"Never mind that. Okay, I found it." Allie opened her phone, only to realize there was no service. "Ugh! I forgot—there's no service here," she groaned in frustration.

She sat down, trying to remember which way they had left the cave that morning. As she thought, she watched Silverspark nosing through her backpack, spilling its contents onto the dirt.

"Silverspark? Are you looking for something?" Allie asked as she continued sifting through her things.

"Yes. I smell food, and I'm hungry," Silverspark replied. She nudged something with her nose, and a sudden crackling sound startled them both.

"My walkie-talkie! Thank you, Silverspark!" Allie exclaimed, rushing over to her scattered belongings. She grabbed the walkie-talkie and quickly tuned it to Stella's station. Silverspark slowly approached, watching her curiously.

"Silverspark to Seaspring. Do you read me? Over," Allie said into the walkie-talkie.

"But I'm not calling! You are. Why did you say my name?" Silverspark asked, puzzled.

"Stella and I made code names after we met all of you..." Allie began, but a burst of static from the walkie-talkie interrupted her.

"Seaspring to Silverspark. I read you loud and clear. Where are you? Over," Stella's voice crackled from the other end.

"We've made contact with them!" Allie exclaimed, dumping the remaining contents of her backpack onto the ground.

"We had to go back to the cave because I forgot my backpack. Amber gave me a book, and we're going to stay here to do some recon. Is everyone on your end safe? Over."

As she waited for Stella to respond, Allie picked up the key from the ground and unlocked the book Amber had given her. She turned to page 87, ready to read, when she heard Stella's voice come through the walkie-talkie.

"Yes, we're all safe. A few minutes ago, we noticed you weren't here and decided to stop. Are you okay? Over."

"Yes, Silverspark and I are in the clearing in front of the cave."

"Tell Amber, we got the book open and are staying here to find the Ira plant that infected Seaspring last night. Do you know where you are? Can you make it back to the cave? Over."

"Ira plant?" Silverspark asked.

"It's a plant that must have infected Seaspring last night. The scent is deadly to small animals but to dragons and other large animals it make this incredibly angry. Thankfully Seaspring only caught a whiff of it but it still effected her."

"Okay, but why do we need to find it? She's fine now, right?" Silverspark questioned

She opened the book, and Silverspark settled behind her, peering at the page. "Not exactly. She might experience aftershocks of anger—some could be even more dangerous than last night. The only way to prevent this is to find the plant and combine it with the mist from a waterfall in the heart of Spring Valley." Allie picked up the walkie-talkie again.

"Stella, can you ask Amber where Spring Valley is? Over." For some reason, she dropped the code names.

"Yes, we can make it back. We're on our way. Over." Stella ended the call without answering Allie's last question. That's when Allie received a call on a different channel.

"Allie, do you read me? This is your brother. We saw your note the morning you left, and it's been crazy ever since. Mom is scared and confused, and so is Dad. Can you please come home? Over." Jacob's voice crackled through. He was in college but must have returned when he heard she was missing. If Allie was honest with herself, she missed him and the rest of her family too.

She sighed as she picked up the walkie-talkie and pressed the button to respond. She knew that once anyone made contact with her, there would be no turning back. But she also knew she had to do it.

"Jacob, I hear you. Please don't tell Mom and Dad that you've made contact with me. They might freak out even more. I want you to know that I'm safe, and I really wish you were here. Over." Allie felt tears welling up.

"Allie! I'm so glad you're safe. But where are you? Over."

"You're never going to believe it, but... I'm in a different world. Over."

Silence.

She slowly set the walkie-talkie down.

"Who was that, Allie?" Silverspark asked.

"My brother. Come on, we have to find the Ira plant."

They got up and began searching, but Allie's mind was elsewhere. She reminisced about the adventures she and Jacob used to pretend they were on. On his last day before college, they had tried to get lost in the woods, but it didn't work—they knew that forest too well. She knew Jacob still longed for a real adventure and was probably feeling sad that she was out here while he was stuck at home with their stressed-out parents. Allie glanced down at the book, hoping it held a way to bring her brother to her. That's when she spotted the portal plant on page 43 of Amber's book.

The page indicated that if you found the plant, you could transport anything or anyone to any place—once per leaf.

If I find that plant, then Jacob could come here, and he could be on a real adventure!

"Silverspark! You go find the Ira plant, and I'll search for the Portal Plant!" Allie shouted as she ran toward the trees leading to the river.

"What? What do you mean by the Portal Plant? Allie!" Silverspark's voice faded into the distance.

Allie was determined to get her brother there. She glanced around and spotted a stream with a river a few miles down. The book mentioned that the plants were mostly found near riverbanks and were easy to identify because they were pink. Allie hoped the book included streams as well.

She hopped into the stream, transformed into a fish, and swam downstream in search of the plant. She didn't realize how far she'd gone until she felt the tug of an undertow, which spit her out into the river. Just as she considered turning back and giving up, she spotted a flash of pink. She swam over and grabbed an entire branch in her mouth. The book said each leaf provided a transport, but she wanted as many chances as possible. She swam back with the plant, then emerged from the stream, transformed back into herself, and dashed to the clearing with the branch.

"There you are! I found the Ira plant! I even had time to put it in the falls. You didn't need to ask Amber—it was right at the end of this stream," Silverspark said, lying in the clearing.

"Great! I found the Portal Plant," Allie said as she walked over to her walkie-talkie and switched to her brother's channel.

"Jacob, do you hear me? Over." She received an immediate response.

"Yes, I read you loud and clear. Over."

"Okay, there's a plant here that can transport things and people, so I'm going to try to bring you here. I need you to pack your travel backpack with everything you think you'll need. I'll transport you in ten minutes, so make sure the backpack is on your back by then. And don't forget good shoes—you won't need food. Got it? Over."

"Yes! I'll be ready in ten minutes!" Jacob exclaimed, his excitement evident as he momentarily forgot to say "over."

Ten minutes later, Allie took a leaf and following the instructions in the book, she wished her brother was there. She opened her eyes when she heard Silverspark start to growl.

"Don't hurt me!" Jacob yelled. Allie turned to see Silverspark baring her teeth at him.

"No, Silverspark!" she called, rushing over to her dragon.

"Allie, do you know him?" Silverspark asked, looking past her.

"Yes, he's my brother!" Allie exclaimed.

"Oh, sorry. He just startled me," Silverspark said.

Allie took a deep breath, then ran to hug her brother. Releasing him, she turned to address both of them.

"Jacob, this is Silverspark. Silverspark, this is Jacob," she said, standing between them as an awkward silence settled in.

"Allie, is that a dragon?" Jacob asked, his eyes wide with disbelief.

"Yes, this is Silverspark, my dragon. She's a Cloud Dragon."

Silverspark turned her nose up in disgust. "Excuse me, a Lightning Cloud Dragon," she corrected.

But just as she spoke, Allie spotted Bloodwing, Stella, and Seaspring approaching through the trees.

"Silverspark, they're back! They found us!" Allie ran over and began explaining the Ira plant to Seaspring, urging her to eat it. Then she started to share about Jacob but stopped short.

In her excitement to see them, Allie was blinded to the fact that they were covered in blood and wore long faces. Then, with horror, she realized Amber wasn't with them.

"Guys…" she asked slowly, dreading the response. "What happened? And where's Amber?"

Chapter 13

There was silence before Stella answered.

"We were attacked by a pack of Wolf Cats. Amber fought them off with her sword and killed two of them. That's where the blood comes from. It's not ours. But.." Bloodwing cut her off.

"But then the last one grabbed Amber by the arm and dragged her through the trees. I ran after them, but they were too fast. It's my fault." He lay down and started to cry.

"No! Amber can't be gone!" Allie cried, looking at Stella, whose cheeks were streaked with tears. Allie felt her own tears starting to fall as they were all overcome with grief.

"Oh, right." Allie suddenly remembered that Jacob was standing there. She didn't want to talk just then, but she needed to explain where this stranger came from. "This is my brother, Jacob. I found the Portal Plant and transported him here. Sorry, Jacob, our friend..." Allie couldn't finish the sentence.

"It's okay, Allie. I heard. Rest in peace, Amber," Jacob said awkwardly.

"Who said anything about being dead?"

They all turned to see Amber enter the clearing, riding on the back of a midnight blue dragon.

"Amber!" Stella and Allie rushed over to her. She hopped off the dragon and ran to meet them. Everyone except Jacob and the new dragon bombarded her with questions.

"Okay, hold on—let me tell you what happened. As I was being dragged away from Bloodwing, I kept seeing a dragon shape above me, which I thought was Bloodwing. But when the Wolf Cat took me to a clearing, another dragon swooped down and killed the cat in one swift motion. That's when I realized it wasn't Bloodwing. The dragon turned around and sat down in front of me. I cautiously introduced myself, and he responded, saying he was DarkIce, an Ice Cloud Dragon. He took me to where I last saw all of you, and then we followed your tracks here.

"So you're telling me we now have another Cloud Dragon?" Allie asked, thinking that their problem of getting Jacob to come with them was solved.

"Yes..." Amber replied, unsure of Allie's excitement.

"That's perfect!" Allie exclaimed, getting up to approach Jacob. She pulled out a small piece of Sugar Puff plant that she had forgotten about in her bag and handed it to him. "Take this to DarkIce."

"Wait! Who are you exactly?" Amber asked, jumping up and drawing her sword, pointing it at his neck.

"Amber, that's my brother," Allie said with a slight sigh. He's obviously safe if everyone is talking to him.

"Yes, please don't kill me," Jacob said, as if he had just noticed how intense the situation was.

"But how did he get here? Did you use the Portal Plant?" Amber asked Allie, still reluctant to lower her sword.

"Yes, I used a Portal Plant. Now can you please put your sword away?" Allie replied, getting straight to the point.

"Fine." Amber slid her sword back into its sheath. "Now we need to go soon. Allie, remember you have to find Sephtis before sundown in two days."

"That's right. Come on, everyone!" Silverspark urged.

Amber, Stella, and Allie jumped onto their dragons.

"Give the plant to DarkIce and meet us down the trail," Allie called over her shoulder to Jacob.

Five minutes later, she turned to see Jacob riding behind her on DarkIce.

"Hi, DarkIce. I'm Allie."

"Nice to meet you, Allie. But can you tell me what's going on?" he asked.

"I'll tell you what—we have a lot to do and discuss, and at sunset, I promise we'll tell you and Jacob everything tonight. But right now, our mission is to get out of the Walk. We don't want to be here after dark—it was lucky Bloodwing found a cave last night." She turned back around.

"Silverspark, go catch up to Bloodwing. I need to ask him something."

She moved to the side of the trail and walked around Seaspring, falling back in line behind Bloodwing. Allie told Seaspring that she just needed to ask Bloodwing something and then they would catch up.

"Bloodwing, can you tell me where you're planning to camp tonight?" Allie asked.

"It depends on how much ground we cover. I want to camp at the base of the first mountain of the Snow Cap Peaks, but with our extra member, we might only make it to Memory Lake. Can you ask everyone if we can speed it up?"

"Of course," Allie replied.

Everyone agreed to speed things up, so Bloodwing led them all in a sprint through the remainder of the Walk. Within about an hour, they were quickly out of the Walk and Willows Wood. They took a break for food and water, and now that they were free from the Walk, they were all eager to fly.

"I'm not so sure I can fly on a dragon yet," Jacob said anxiously. But it was too late; they needed to hurry.

"Don't worry. If you fall, I'll catch you before you hit the ground," DarkIce assured him.

"Okay." Gulp. "Let's do this, I guess," Jacob said.

They all lifted off, soaring toward the Snow Cap Peaks. Allie loved the feeling of being in the air again; she was tired of being stuck on the ground, and she knew everyone else felt the same.

Stella was smiling and laughing as Seaspring flew circles in the air. Amber was looking around with a map in her hands as Bloodwing just glided with his wings not flapping and his eyes closed. And DarkIce and Jacob were having a long conversation. Allie looked down at Silverspark and noticed she was staring at the tallest mountain of Snow Cap Peaks.

"Silverspark, what are you looking at?" Allie asked.

"There's a storm brewing on the other side of the mountain. We might need to reach the Shadow of the Moon today; the storm will hit tonight. Alternatively, we could wait until dusk and go around it, traveling through the mountains and finishing our journey tomorrow." Silverspark turned and announced this to the others.

"Well, that's perfect for Allie. She needs to find Sephtis tomorrow before midnight," Amber said.

"Okay, but can we stop at Memory Lake? Being cooped up in the Walk wore me out," Bloodwing grunted, giving an extra flap of his wings.

"Sure, we can stop for a few hours until dusk. We'll set out again at dawn and—"

"Sure, but promise to tell me what's happening when we get to the lake?" Jacob and DarkIce said in unison.

"Yes!" everyone replied. Then there was a moment of silence before they all burst into uncontrollable laughter— the kind that comes from being so tired and anxious that it spills out in gasps.

They flew to Memory Lake, landing on the first bank they reached. Amber jumped off Bloodwing and led him to the water.

"Okay, we need to rest up quickly—" Amber began, but she was cut off.

"Thank you, Amber! But we can take care of ourselves, so let's get a camp started," Seaspring said. Stella and Allie exchanged glances; that level of sass was completely unexpected from Seaspring.

Stella walked over to Seaspring. "Hey, girl, are you okay?"

While they talked, Allie shifted her attention back to the others.

They were staring at her with confusion, and Allie noticed Amber looking at her with hurt in her eyes. This surprised her; she hadn't seen anything affect Amber so deeply since they met. They stood in silence, the faint sound of Stella and Seaspring talking on the shoreline nearby.

"We need to start a fire, so..." Everyone finally understood and moved on.

Later that night, after they had built a fire, they began to tell Jacob and DarkIce what had happened and what they needed to do.

"So, long story short, five days ago I discovered I can shapeshift, and I had to travel to a different world to find someone named Sephtis to remove his enchantment from me. Stella and I did some research based on a campfire story Dad told us—that's how we knew about this in the first place—and then we found the portal. Then we met Amber, who had a very unique story that was tied to mine, so she decided to join us. We invited her because she has lived here all her life and knows almost everything."

"Then we met the dragons and really began our quest through Misty Meadows and Willows Wood. We ended up having to go through the Walk because of a storm—that's where you came in. Now we have only two more days, including what's left of today, to reach the Shadow of the Moon in the Snow Cap Peaks and find Sephtis."

When Allie finished, both Jacob and DarkIce were staring at her with their mouths open, trying to comprehend everything she had just explained. Seaspring reached over with the tips of her wings and gently closed their mouths.

"So you mean to tell me that you can shapeshift?" Jacob asked excitedly.

"Yes, she can shapeshift," Bloodwing confirmed. "Now, you tell me how you came across Amber in the woods." Bloodwing's deep tone made it sound like he was accusing DarkIce of treason.

"I was on my way back to Misty Meadows from a visit with my friends in the Peaks when I heard growling and screaming," DarkIce said matter-of-factly.

"Oh, okay." Bloodwing backed off. "Well, we need to get going now; we've rested enough."

"Wait, we don't have to leave yet. I mean, if Allie has two more days to search in the Peaks, then we don't have to go right now, right?" DarkIce asked.

"No. We want to get this over with as quickly as possible. Besides, the mountain range is huge! It could take two days to find Sephtis," Amber said as she climbed onto Bloodwing's back.

"Okay, but can I see Allie shapeshift first?" DarkIce asked.

"Sure, I guess. I don't use it that much because I really like it and don't want to lose it, but yes," she replied. It was true; she didn't want to lose her power, but she knew it was the only way.

She transformed into a lion, and as soon as she did, DarkIce screamed and yelled at her before running behind a bush like a coward. Everyone was left confused by his reaction. Allie had encountered scared reactions before, but none quite like that. She turned back into herself and ran over to DarkIce in the bushes.

"DarkIce! I'm so sorry if I scared you! I didn't mean to!" Allie exclaimed.

"Allie? Oh, it's okay. Sorry, I thought—well, I'm scared of lions," he admitted.

"It's okay, and I'm sorry. I didn't know. But we need to get back to the others and start flying." She led him back to the group, and in silence, they took to the air. Once they were airborne, they decided to climb higher. Bloodwing led them straight to the highest clouds.

"Now, let me warn you, it gets really hard to fly up there. Bloodwing fell out of the sky the first time we tried to fly in the Jet Streams," Seaspring said as they climbed higher.

"Excuse me? That's true, but you did too! So, slow down," Bloodwing replied defensively.

"Wait. You said Jet Streams? I wouldn't have thought this place had jets. It doesn't seem like somewhere with high technology," Jacob said, a suspicious look on his face.

"No, we don't have jets—whatever those are. We call them Jet Streams because when you hit the right stream of air, you jet through the sky, cutting about three hours off your travel time. The hard part is finding the right one; there's a stream for every direction," Seaspring explained.

"Oh," Jacob said, his face heating up with embarrassment.

They stopped in the open air, and Silverspark told Allie that they had arrived. Amber began waving her arms around as if swatting at flies.

"Amber... you okay?" Stella asked. "What are you doing?"

"I'm trying—*grunt*—to find the—*grunt*—Jet Stream! Ah, found it!" She sat back down on Bloodwing and directed him toward the stream.

As soon as Silverspark entered the Jet Stream, Allie felt a surge of movement pulling her toward the Peaks. The Jet Stream was a force like nothing she had ever experienced, propelling them along at record speed. Apparently, the dragons hadn't flown in those Streams before or enogh. From the ground, they looked like giant balls of color tumbling through the air. Allie heard Amber, Stella, and Jacob screaming as they clung on for dear life. She, too, struggled to hold on to Silverspark. She fell off and hung in the air for a moment as the Jet Stream's force carried her along with everyone else. Then, as if an invisible hand had let go, she plummeted out of the Jet Stream. She tried to scream for Silverspark, but her voice failed her. As she fell, she watched her friends shrink smaller and smaller against the sky.

So this is it. I'll never get to Sephtis now.

She thought of all her friends had endured just to help her reach him and be cured.

"Allie."

The voice echoed again. *Who is that? I'm falling in mid-air.*

"Allie."

"Who are you?" she demanded, finally finding her voice. "Where are you?"

The ground rushed closer.

"Allie, use your powers."

Her powers. But it was too late.

She struck the ground with such force that it knocked the breath out of her, plunging her into darkness. She tried to sit up, but the earth seemed to have a grip on her, refusing to let go.

A weak "Help!" was all Allie could muster before she fell face-first into the mud, slipping back into unconsciousness.

Chapter 14

When Allie came back to reality, she remained face-down in the mud. For a long time, she heard nothing around her. She just lay there, gathering the strength to sit up.

"Allie?" A familiar voice called out.

"I saw her go down here, I think," said another voice.

Suddenly, she felt something kick her in the side.

"Hey guys! I found her," the first voice called. Moments later, she felt someone lift her and prop her up against what she thought was a tree stump.

As her vision cleared, Allie noticed three worried faces sitting in front of her. Beyond them, she spotted a large red dragon, a green one, and a dark blue one looming over their shoulders. The tree stump behind her shifted, revealing a fourth silver dragon. Despite recognizing the voices and faces before her, Allie struggled to recall their names, no matter how hard she tried.

"Who are you?" Allie finally asked. The dark blue dragon sighed. "Seriously? You didn't hit the ground so hard that you lost your memory, did you? Drop the act, Allie."

"DarkIce! That's no way to treat my sister," the boy said. The girl with the sword stepped up beside him, adding, "I agree. Calm down, DarkIce."

"You're taking his side?" Allie said, glancing at the sword-bearer. "Are you his girlfriend?" she laughed, noticing the boy's face turn red.

"No, we're just friends," the girl replied, a hint of irritation in her voice. "You're clearly not feeling well, Allie."

"Okay, cool. But I'm your sister?" Allie turned back to the boy, trying to process this new information.

He resembles me, I think, she thought, though it was hard to tell with everyone caked in mud. Allie realized she was the one most covered in it, having been face down just moments before.

"Yes, Allie, I'm Jacob." The moment he spoke his name, a wave of memories washed over her, bringing everything back. Allie turned to Amber.

"Sorry for asking that," she said, referencing the girlfriend question.

"Nah, you're fine. I know you weren't yourself." She hugged Allie. The girl who hadn't spoken yet—Stella—rushed over and embraced her as well. "I'm so glad you're okay," Stella said.

Silverspark looked at Allie. "I nearly had a heart attack when you fell! The moment I lost connection with you, I called everyone else and shot down. We saw you drop below the clouds and couldn't find you—until Jacob kicked you in the side." She nudged Allie playfully. "I'm so glad we found you." Then Allie hugged her tightly.

"What was I in?" Allie asked, glancing back at the pool of mud.

"We're in the Northern Prairies. You just entered the Mud Pots. In this part of the prairie, there are pools of mud everywhere." Amber waved her hand behind her, revealing a vast expanse of Mud Pots—no trees for miles, just grass and mud.

"Well, I, for one, would like to clean up and not have mud caked in my hair for days," Stella said as she climbed onto Seaspring. "Come on, I think I saw a river while we were searching for Allie."

They all mounted their dragons and flew a little longer to the river Stella had spotted. Instead of letting their riders off at the edge, the dragons dove right into the water, clearly eager for them to get clean. As they emerged from the river, DarkIce turned to face them.

"Okay, guys. Hurry up! We need to reach the back of the Peaks before sundown. Just rinse off, and then let's go."

But there were other plans. As Allie was emerging from the river, Jacob sneaked up behind her and pulled her underwater.

As soon as she surfaced, Allie saw Jacob do the same to Stella. She dashed over and pulled him underwater. Stella emerged and raced for

Amber. They continued this playful splash fest until Allie fell back into the water, holding up an imaginary white flag in surrender.

"I can't do this anymore," she said, waving her hands in the air, laughing and breathing heavily.

"Fine. You can dry off. But I still haven't dunked Amber yet. I was scared of that sword, but not anymore!" He dove toward her, but Amber stepped aside easily, and Jacob face-planted in the water.

Allie laughed as she climbed out and tried to wring out her hair. DarkIce approached the river's edge. "Okay, guys, let's go!" he urged, sounding very persistent.

"Fine, even though I still haven't dunked Amber—but fine." Jacob climbed out of the river and turned to help Stella and Amber.

"Now we've just lost fifteen critical moments. Can we please—" DarkIce was interrupted by Silverspark stepping up. "DarkIce! Leave them alone! It's okay for them to have some fun."

He looked down. "I'm sorry, you're right. I just want to get there, you know?" He looked apologetic, but his tone didn't quite match.

"It's okay, buddy. I know we all want to reach Sephtis. Come on, let's go now." Jacob hopped onto DarkIce's back.

Once they had all mounted, the dragons soared across the Northern Prairies toward the Peaks again. A storm was brewing near Mount Tyrick, the tallest mountain on the southern side of the Peaks.

"Uh-oh. We might get hit by another storm if we don't make it there tonight. Come on, let's pick up the pace!" Seaspring dove forward, and the others followed suit.

"Okay, we need to make camp here. We can find Sephtis in the morning." Allie surveyed the tired faces around her; everyone had already fallen asleep.

"Well, I guess it's just us who need to go to sleep now, right, Silverspark?" she said with a chuckle. But when she turned around, she saw that Silverspark was already asleep, too.

As Allie lay down, she reflected on all the days that had passed—from the first day she discovered her powers to this moment, lying down with her friends. She couldn't believe what they had endured to help her find Sephtis. Excitement bubbled within her at the thought of finally going home to see her parents. But one question lingered: *What was that voice calling her name?*

It was a voice unlike any she had ever heard—smooth like a river yet commanding. Just by its tone, she knew that whatever it spoke was true. She felt a strange familiarity with it, not in a direct way, but as if it resonated within her heart.

She drifted off to sleep, the unanswered question still lingering in her mind as her friends rested nearby.

The next morning, when Allie woke up, everyone was already up and packed.

"Come on, Allie, we were just about to wake you!" Stella said, handing her backpack to her.

"Wait, guys, where's DarkIce?" Jacob asked, scanning the area.

That's when they all realized DarkIce was gone. Allie spent a few minutes searching for him with the others until she remembered she needed to finish packing from the night.

"Shh, what's that sound?" Seaspring raised her head, tilting it to listen as the noise grew closer. It sounded like metal.

"Hide," she whispered.

They all dashed for the bushes just as a band of dragons entered the clearing. But these weren't Cloud Dragons; they were red, both male and female. Their horns looked sharp enough to spear right through you, and they were covered in black "armor." The armor on their bodies extended to their tails and featured sharp spikes. The facial armor surrounded their eyes and extended down to their noses, stopping just above their upper lips. Following the swirling patterns on their horns, a single strip of metal wrapped around each one.

"Okay, but why did Sephtis send us here with the blue one?" one dragon asked.

"Don't say that when he's around! He's Sephtis's second-in-command, aside from Siege. You know you'd be killed for that. DarkIce would cut off your wings and throw you off the cliff into the ocean."

They all exchanged glances. DarkIce? Second-in-command to Sephtis?

"Yeah, I know. But still, why?" the first dragon pressed.

"Ugh! There's a group of humans and Cloud Dragons here looking for Sephtis. We're here to escort them," another dragon replied, laughing.

The entire group erupted in laughter at the mention of "escort."

"So what are we waiting for?"

"You're waiting for me, my fellow Blood Rippers." DarkIce emerged into the clearing, wearing the same armor as the others.

"No, DarkIce," Jacob said.

"You weren't going to have all the fun of chaining them without me, were you, Stripesun?" DarkIce snarled.

"No, Commander DarkIce. My deepest apologies, sir," Stripesun said, bowing deeply.

"Now, Bloodwing! I know you are here. Come out or I'll kill Seaspring."

Chapter 15

Bloodwing came bounding out of the bushes, charging at DarkIce. Amber tried to scream, but Jacob quickly grabbed her and covered her mouth before they could find the others.

Bloodwing was about to reach DarkIce when a net flew out, sending him crashing to the ground. He struggled for a moment until one of the guards approached, tied his wings to his sides, chained his front paws, and secured the ends of the chains to a nearby tree.

"Now, Bloodwing, be a good dragon and stay there," DarkIce said, walking over to him. He slid his sharp claw down Bloodwing's neck just enough to make him cringe.

Amber stared in shook that her dragon was taken down so easily. A single tear dripped down her check onto the grass. Suddenly, Bloodwing unleashed a blast of fire toward DarkIce, who jumped back and shouted, "Now!" In a flash, Seaspring and Silverspark leaped out from the bushes, unleashing blasts at the guards.

Amber emerged as well, wielding her sword and working to free Bloodwing from the chains that bound him. The first thing that came to Allie's mind was a phoenix. She transformed into one, igniting in flames as she began blasting the armed Blood Rippers. Even Stella joined in, swinging a stick to fend off the dragons.

At the same time, the Blood Rippers began attacking. While Allie soared through the air, she caught sight of a swirl of colors, accompanied by a sound that was one of the most terrifying she had ever heard. The screams of the two or three Blood Rippers who fell to Silverspark's lighting mingled with the clash of metal on metal, followed by the shriek as Silverspark was ensnared by one of the nets.

Allie dove to free her, but she too was caught by the nets. That's when she noticed one of the dragons hovering above, dropping the nets down on them.

Once she realized that, Allie saw that Stella, Amber, and Seaspring had all been caught in nets as well.

"Where did this firebird come from?" one of the guards still standing asked, panting for breath.

"That's not a firebird. Allie, come on, it's over. Change back to yourself," DarkIce said as she transformed back into her human form.

The Blood Rippers gasped.

"Yes this is the one Sephtis wants." DarkIce said to the group of dragons. "Now hold on, there is one more." He walked over to the bushes they had been hiding in and grabbed Jacob by the collar of his shirt.

"Why are you doing this?" Jacob demanded.

"I'll explain on the way. Now, chain them up!" DarkIce commanded.

The dragons placed shackles around the wrists of Amber, Stella, Jacob, and Allie, and secured them to the front claws of Bloodwing, Silverspark, and Seaspring.

Linked by chains, they marched in a line, Jacob leading the way and Bloodwing bringing up the rear. Surrounded by the Blood Rippers, they felt like prisoners on their way to Sephtis. Their mission was clear—they were to meet Sephtis—but doubts began to creep in, leaving them wondering if they had made a grave mistake.

"So, you want an explanation?" DarkIce chuckled. "You fell perfectly for my little lie about where I'd been and how I found Amber! It was brilliant!" He laughed so hard that he tumbled to the ground, rolling with glee. By the time he finally regained his composure, the group had moved past him.

He rushed to catch up with them. "I assume you've heard that I'm Sephtis's second-in-command. I've always served his majesty faithfully. When he learned that Allie was in this world, he sent me to retrieve her and bring her back. Just as I passed the D-Gate, he called me back."

"He told me to wait until little Amber was with her," he sneered at Amber. "So I waited. When his majesty summoned me, I brought you to my troops. Now, all we have to do is reach the Crescent Fortress—or as you call it, the Shadow of the Moon." He laughed uproariously as realization spread across their faces.

"So the Shadow of the Moon is actually a fortress?" Stella asked.

"Yes. It's where Sephtis resides and where all his troops are stationed. Why do you think it's visible during the day?" he replied, raising an eyebrow.

The more he spoke and connected the dots, the more Allie felt foolish for missing the obvious clues.

"So wait, what's the D-Gate?" Amber asked.

"What do you think the 'D' stands for, Amber?" he replied mockingly.

Amber turned ghostly pale, and Allie's heart sank as she realized with horror that they were heading toward a Death Gate.

"If Sephtis is this horrible creature, why would he heal me?" Allie asked, fear creeping into her voice as she awaited his response.

He laughed derisively. "You foolish little human, he won't heal you! He placed that enchantment to gather more followers. And he's not a horrible creature—he is the king of this realm!" DarkIce proclaimed.

They had been traveling for hours, and with each ascent, the cold intensified. Snow blanketed the ground, and Allie's hands had turned blue, but the Blood Rippers drove them onward. Occasionally, someone would slip on a patch of ice and fall, but still, they pressed ahead.

It wasn't night yet; in fact, it was the hottest part of the day, yet the cold still clung to them. When Allie looked back at Silverspark and the dragons, she saw their wings frozen to their sides. Allie couldn't comprehend how the Blood Rippers seemed unfazed by the cold, showing no signs of discomfort.

Allie recognized the dragon Stripesun next to her. Gathering her courage, she asked, "Why aren't you cold? It's freezing!" Her teeth chattered as she spoke.

Stripesun didn't answer. Instead, her entire body ignited, blazing like a walking fireball.

The warmth of the fire slowly spread through Allie's body, making it easier for her to walk faster and keep up with the dragon. The only downside to having a fire dragon beside her was that the snow turned to slush beneath her feet, making it difficult to maintain her balance.

Allie glanced back, expecting to see Amber, chained behind her, slipping in the slush. Instead, Amber was walking on solid snow. It seemed the cold was so intense that once the snow and ice moved away from the heat, they refroze instantly.

"Good idea, Stripesun! Everyone else, flame up! Let's refreeze the snow and cover our tracks, so 'He' can't find us," DarkIce called from the front. Allie noticed that DarkIce was freezing just like she had been, as he was a Cloud Dragon, unlike the fiery red dragons surrounding them.

With the dragons providing warmth, the last few hours hadn't been so bad. But just as Allie began to feel somewhat calm, they rounded a corner and suddenly faced what had to be the Death Gate. The dragons pressed on, unfazed, while Stella, Amber, Jacob, Bloodwing, Seaspring, Silverspark, and Allie stared at the gate, terror etched on their faces.

The gate was completely black. Since the fortress took the shape of a circle, the fence surrounding the forest curved away from them, making the gate appear larger than it actually was.

As soon as the dragons moved away, the cold hit them hard, forcing them to sprint toward the warmth, even if it meant getting closer to the gate.

Once they passed through, the doors swung shut behind them as if on their own. Just a few feet from the fence stood the real door of the fortress, guarded by two more Blood Rippers.

They pushed open the massive gray doors and stepped into a dark hallway.

The hallway was tall and winding, with only torches lining the walls for light. Once inside, the dragons extinguished their flames, and a chill returned, though it was not uncomfortably cold. An eerie silence enveloped them.

"Welcome to the Shadow of the Moon," DarkIce said.

Allie tried to keep track of their turns, hoping to remember the way out, but frustration quickly set in. There was no way anyone could find the exit once they entered; every hallway looked just like the last.

They approached another door, and when it opened, they found themselves staring down a set of spiral stairs. The stairwell was wide enough for the dragons to fly down, so they took off, hovering beside the others who had to walk. The tight curve of the stairs made it difficult for Bloodwing, Seaspring, and Silverspark to navigate their descent.

They were careful not to get too close to the center of the spiral, where sharp pieces of metal and glass jutted out. It was clear that every aspect of this fortress was designed to torture prisoners.

When they reached the bottom, they entered another door leading into a second hallway. This one was different from the main hall; the torches were spaced farther apart, and in between them were barred doors leading to cells. Some cells were empty, while others held creatures whose faces were filled with terror, sadness, and hopelessness.

They were taken to the last door and thrown into two separate cells on opposite sides of the hallway. One cell contained Amber, Stella, Jacob, and Allie, while the dragons were in the other. Stripesun approached, removed their chains, and secured the doors once they were inside.

"Now then, don't get too comfy. I'm guessing that as soon as I inform Sephtis you're here, he'll be requesting your presence." With that, DarkIce and the Blood Rippers walked back down the hallway and shut the door.

Chapter 16

"I'm sorry, guys. Maybe if I hadn't run out when DarkIce called me, we wouldn't be in this mess," Bloodwing said.

"No, Bloodwing, it's not your fault. We would have ended up here anyway, even if we had stuck to our plan. You know that," Allie replied.

"I know, but I still blame myself." Bloodwing went to sit in the corner of the dragon's cell.

While Silverspark and Seaspring tried to comfort Bloodwing, the others engaged in quiet conversation as well.

"There's one thing I still don't understand: how can Sephtis be this great king and have so many followers if he's truly this horrible beast?" Stella asked.

They sat in silence, each lost in their own thoughts. *That's true.*

Why is Sephtis supposed to heal my powers? Was this all a trick to lure us in? DarkIce's words echoed in Allie's mind: "Ha ha. He won't heal you!"

"Sorry I brought you along on this," she said to Jacob, her head down. "You could be at home with Mom and Dad instead of in this cell."

"No, Allie, I wouldn't give this up for anything. Besides, if you hadn't brought me here, we would have never gotten this plant." To Allie, it didn't feel like he was right next to her.

Suddenly, they all looked up to see Jacob standing between the cells.

"What? You didn't think I would give up, did you?" He held up the Portal Plant, and Allie recalled that it had been in her backpack the whole time.

"I found it in your backpack, which I'm glad they didn't take. Now come on, there are exactly enough leaves for each of us. Everyone take a leaf." He distributed leaves to Amber, Allie, Stella, and the dragons. "Just close your eyes and wish to be next to me."

Once they were all in the hallway, Amber used her sword to cut the ropes binding the dragons' wings.

"Alright, I think I remember the way out. Follow me." Amber began walking down the hallway and opened the door to the stairs. She turned around to see the others still standing in front of the cells and motioned for them to follow.

They ascended the stairs while the dragons flew, just as DarkIce and the others had done on the way down. Once everyone reached the top, Amber looked back, and Stella and Allie nodded at her.

She slowly opened the door, which squeaked loudly, causing everyone to freeze. They stood there, listening. Silence.

Amber poked her head out, then slid out and signaled that it was safe. Once they were all in the hallway, they realized they needed to solve the flying problem. Once they exited the fortress, they would want to go straight up to get out of range and then head anywhere but there.

"We can all get on the dragons, but what about Jacob?" Stella said.

"Why don't you all get on the dragons now? Jacob, you can ride Silverspark. I'll turn into a bird or something and fly alongside you."

"Actually," Allie said, considering the possibilities, "why don't I change into Stripesun right now? That way, if we run into a guard, we'll be ready." She transformed into Stripesun, and everyone else instinctively fell into line behind her.

As they walked down the hall, Amber, positioned right behind Allie, directed her. Allie genuinely believed they could pass by a guard by claiming they were her prisoners.

They had been walking down the hallway for what felt like ages. Allie was growing increasingly uncertain that they would make it out. She didn't remember it taking this long to get in.

"This doesn't feel right," Allie said just as a guard came around the corner.

"Stripesun, what are you doing?" he asked.

"I'm taking these prisoners back to their cells. They tried to escape, but I caught them," she replied, trying to keep her tone matter-of-fact.

He stepped closer. "Well, you're heading the wrong way. The cells are in the other direction."

"Are you sure?" Allie asked, unsure of how to navigate this situation.

"Ugh. No. Stripesun, you know I've only been here for a few days. You know your way around much better than I do. Go on." He stepped aside and allowed them to pass.

Once they rounded the corner and were sure they were out of earshot, Allie turned to the others.

"Whew! That was close! I can't believe we got out of that one," she said, leaning against the wall.

"I know. Once he said the cells were in the other direction, I thought we were caught for sure," Jacob said.

"Well, come on. We'd better keep going. That was a little too close," Amber urged.

"I agree. I think we're almost out. See how the walls are getting wider? I remember them narrowing as we came in, so I believe we're heading in the right direction," Seaspring said. Allie nodded; the walls were definitely widening.

They walked a bit longer and soon came upon a large door.

"I think we did it! This has to be the way out!" Silverspark said excitedly.

Allie nudged the door open with her nose and nearly fell forward, bursting into tears. As she peered through the crack, instead of seeing the outdoors, she found herself looking into a large room. It was bright, with a long gray rug stretching from the door to a black throne at the far end. Sitting on the throne was none other than Sephtis himself.

"Ahh. Took you long enough, Allie Kate," Sephtis said, locking his gaze on her with an evil yet satisfied grin.

He jumped off his throne, walked to the door, opened it fully, and then sat back down. "Come in, come in! Don't be shy. I'm so sorry if my guards scared you. I told them not to put you in the cells, but, as always, they didn't listen," Sephtis said.

None of them trusted him at all; they all stood just outside the door.

"Okay, I tried," Sephtis continued in his overly kind, 'I'm totally not going to hurt you' voice.

He jumped up, getting so close that Allie could see a sliver of white in his black and red eyes.

"Come in. That is not a request!" he demanded, his tone shifting to what sounded like his real voice—deep and terrifying.

They slowly slipped inside, Sephtis's piercing red eyes watching them intently. Once they were all in, he closed the doors behind them and returned to his throne.

Only now did she realize that his black sludge-colored mane moved like real fire. It seemed to follow the direction he moved, swaying and flickering a moment after he did.

"Now, Allie. Change into yourself," he commanded, boring his eyes into her. When she complied, he remained unfazed, not even looking pleased.

Two Blood Rippers approached and chained them to the ground where they stood. Then a small door, which Allie hadn't noticed before, opened, and a stream of strange creatures poured out—beings unlike anything they had ever seen.

Each creature had greenish-gray skin that appeared covered in slime. They all had large ears protruding from the sides of their heads. The females sported long black hair that trailed on the ground, while the males were completely bald. All of them wore what looked like dusty, stained, and even torn tablecloths. The girls' hair was so matted that it resembled long mops more than actual hair.

As the three-foot-tall creatures approached, the two Blood Rippers glanced at Sephtis, who nodded, giving them permission to unleash fire on any creature that didn't move quickly enough. The "Hexies," as Sephtis called them, shoved cloth into the prisoners' mouths, silencing them, then scurried back through the door to avoid the laughter of the Blood Rippers, who were now rolling on the floor in amusement.

"You foolish child," Sephtis said, locking his gaze on Allie. "DarkIce informed me that you asked if I was going to heal you." Sephtis menacing laugh echoed in the room.

"Of course I won't heal you! It was just to get you here! You were a fool to believe such a thing! But, I knew you would come. Since all humans are little fools. "And now, he can't get to you. He can't steal you and twist your minds! You are safe here. And here you will stay!"

"Now, Amber, I still can't believe you didn't come to me sooner. I've been waiting for the day when Amber would finally be MINE!" Sephtis's deep, evil laughter filled the room.

"AND THE REST OF YOU ARE JUST AN ADDED BONUS!" he said with a satisfied smile.

Chapter 17

"Ever since I failed to conquer the other realm, He banished me here. I've been here ever since, gathering an army to reclaim what is rightfully mine! Now, leave me!" Sephtis yelled.

Suddenly, the ceiling above them began to shake. Dust and debris filled the air as the room trembled violently, and cracks spidered across the ceiling. With a final bang, it burst open, sending a cloud of dust and metal swirling. Light flooded in from the opening, revealing a herd of white-winged horses led by a lion cub. Sephtis screamed, and in response, a legion of Blood Rippers charged at their attackers.

Allie and her friends were caught in the chaos. Unable to move, Allie closed her eyes, overwhelmed by the sounds of battle all around her.

She was struck on the cheek by a dragon's claw and kicked in the back by a horse. For a brief moment, she felt the heat as a Blood Ripper's flame engulfed her, and when she opened her eyes, she saw that the sleeve of her shirt was gone. Meanwhile, Stella had a clear view of the main battle.

Sephtis and the lion cub were locked in battle on the throne platform. Sephtis leaped and lunged, trying to attack the lion cub, who simply yawned and stood there. Each time Sephtis struck, his paw bounced off, leaving the cub completely unharmed.

The battle seemed to progress rapidly. Soon, almost all the Blood Rippers had either fled, been injured or died. Most of the horses remained, still trying to take down the last few dragons. Realizing he couldn't harm the lion, Sephtis gave up and turned his attention to attacking the pegasi.

The cub bounded over to them. When he got close, all of the chains holding them down disappeared and so did their gags.

"Each of you, mount a horse. Bloodwing, Seaspring and Silverspark follow us." It spoke in a gentle and calm voice. Shocked by the fact the little lion spoke, and knew their names, it took them a second to comply.

Once they recovered from their shock, Amber, Stella, Jacob, and Allie each mounted a pegasi. As soon as they were settled, they took to the sky, followed by Bloodwing, Seaspring, Silverspark, and the cub. While they flew away, Allie heard Sephtis's deep, angry scream and the roars of the Blood Rippers behind them.

"Now you are safe, and we're on our way to the true King. Allie, he is waiting to heal you. Amber, he will explain everything. And for the rest of you, he is home."

"Who are you, and how do we know this 'king' will do what he says?" Stella asked.

"My name is Camino. I am the Son of King Amar. Sephtis is the author of confusion and the king of lies; he had no intention of telling you the truth or healing you. However, King Amar will provide you with the truth and do what is best for you."

The moment Allie heard that name, she felt a sense of peace wash over her. Though she had never heard it before, it felt oddly familiar.

Camino led the winged horses down through the clouds. Once they broke through, everyone gasped at the breathtaking view. It was as if they had entered an entirely different realm. The air here felt similar to Earth's, but it was imbued with a sense of peace and joy. Before them lay pure, green rolling hills, forming a valley at the center. At the end of the valley stood a beautiful castle.

The castle was a brilliant white and gold, featuring seven tall towers at the back. In front, a grand courtyard stretched out, visible from miles away. The castle had a radiant glow that made it seem to shine even from a distance. It was a far more welcoming sight than the Crescent Fortress.

Along the hills and through the valley lay a magnificent golden road, with villages stretching as far as the eye could see on either side. The villages only enhanced the beauty of the scene.

Camino led the horses to the golden road that wound through the valley. As they arrived, many villagers came out to greet the horses, and to Allie's surprise, they welcomed her and the others as well.

She heard phrases like, "How was your flight?" "Do you need any water?" "Would you like something to eat?" and "Are you on your way to the castle?" The friendly faces surrounded them, and a lively buzz of conversation rose from the crowd as everyone mingled and introduced themselves.

A little lady approached Allie. She had long gray hair that cascaded down to her hips. She wore glasses, and was dressed in a lovely spring dress with a dark green drape over her shoulders.

"Do you need a place to sleep tonight? It's almost dusk, and you all will need food," she said kindly, reminding Allie of her grandmother.

Camino approached. "That would be great, Lila. You have my thanks," he said.

"Camino," Allie interjected, "I don't know if you're aware, but tomorrow is the last day for someone to heal me of the enchantment." Although she now understood that Sephtis wouldn't heal her, she still didn't want to turn into him.

"Sister, Sephtis may not have been able to heal you, but the enchantment still lingers. I promise you, healing is coming, and you will emerge better than new." Camino smiled, Allie's eyes sparkled with hope.

Lila led them down a winding path away from town until they reached a quaint cottage nestled in a field, shaded by a grand oak tree.

"Make yourselves comfortable on the grass," she said, darting inside. The grass was surprisingly soft—so soft, in fact, that the dragons rolled about, scratching their backs and soothing their cuts and bruises from their journey. Finally, they lay down, looking thoroughly satisfied.

Lila emerged from the house, balancing a tray with five cups of water for the humans. She hurried back inside, returning three more times, each trip bringing a large bowl filled with water for the dragons. Finally, she came out once more, this time holding a smaller bowl for Camino. Once she finished, Lila sat down and took a refreshing sip of water. "So, what do you all want for dinner?" she asked kindly.

"Well, you wouldn't happen to have any Cloud Puff plants, would you?" Seaspring inquired, a hopeful glint in her eyes.

They all chuckled, realizing the dragons must be starving. It had been days since they'd been near any Cloud Puffs. They had been subsisting on water, berries, and the occasional patch of grass—much to Bloodwing's chagrin, who firmly believed that such fare was a disgrace to all dragons. But it was all they had for now.

Allie felt a wave of happiness at the thought of something other than berries. She couldn't believe Amber had spent years eating just those.

"Actually, we have a field of Cloud Puffs just over that way," Lila said, pointing into the distance. Instantly, the dragons perked up and took off, excitement evident in their swift movements.

They all laughed, sharing in the dragons' excitement. "So, what can I serve you?" Lila asked again, her smile bright.

"We don't want to intrude too much," Amber replied, "so anything you have is great." The others nodded in agreement.

Lila smiled and walked inside, with Camino trailing behind, eager to help. The group sat in silence for a while, reflecting on everything that had just transpired. After a few more moments, they began to share their thoughts, breaking the stillness with quiet conversation.

Amber exclaimed, "I can't believe Sephtis is... well, that!" She let out a sigh of frustration.

"Didn't you say you talked with him through? When you came out of the 'In Between World?'" Stella asked.

"I only talked with him through messengers." Amber said.

"Ok, but how lucky are we that Camino arrived just when he did!" Stella added, her eyes sparkling with excitement.

A buzz of enthusiasm began to build among them.

They still had many questions for Camino, but he assured them they would all be answered the next day. So, they settled into a comfortable rhythm, enjoying their first truly calm conversation since Stella and Allie had entered this world.

Camino and Lila emerged, both carrying trays—Camino balancing his on his back. As they set the trays down, a heavenly aroma wafted over to Allie, making her stomach growl. They enjoyed a delightful meal, sharing warm fellowship with Lila and Camino. Later that night, when the dragons returned, Lila invited them inside, but the dragons were content to stay on the soft, inviting grass.

"No, no! You too, my darlings," Lila insisted.

"Um, we won't fit through the door," Bloodwing said, looking confused.

Lila laughed, a sweet, melodic sound. "Yes, you will! Come and see."

The dragons got up and slowly approached the door. Miraculously, they fit through without shrinking or breaking anything. Once all three dragons were inside, Amber, Jacob, Stella, Allie, and Camino followed, and Lila gently shut the door behind them. Allie expected it to be a tight squeeze, especially since one dragon was nearly as tall as the cottage itself. However, when she stepped inside, she was pleasantly surprised by how spacious it felt.

The inside of the house had designated spots for each dragon to lie down comfortably without disturbing the rest of the space. The girls headed upstairs to the third floor, where each of them had their own complete bedroom, while Jacob's room was on the second floor.

"How is this possible, Lila?" Allie asked, bouncing onto the bed in her room.

"You'll learn more about it tomorrow. This is my power of hospitality," Lila replied with a smile before gently closing the door.

As Allie drifted off to sleep, she felt a sense of peace wash over her, free from fear for the first time in days.

The next morning, as the group prepared to leave, Lila came out to bid them farewell. They expressed their gratitude for her kindness and hospitality.

"Thank you so much, Lila," Stella said, hugging the old lady tightly.

"Of course, dear. Anytime," Lila replied as they started down the road back to the village.

When they arrived at the village to collect their horses, the group was eager to begin their journey to the castle. Amber, Stella, and Allie hopped aboard their dragons, while Jacob mounted a winged horse. As they took to the skies again, Allie glanced down at Silverspark, a mix of awe and anticipation filling her.

"Are you excited?" Allie asked her.

"Yes! I'm so excited! I didn't even know this land existed; otherwise, I would have come here a long time ago."

"I know! When Stella and I did our research before coming here, there was nothing about another realm—no hints at all!" Allie recalled their studies before leaving with Stella. If they had known then what they knew now, they would have never ventured into the Pertiaus Realm.

"Yeah, I was just thinking that," Stella said as she and Seaspring glided over to them.

"I'm ready for some answers too. I have so many questions," Seaspring added.

"They'll all be answered soon, sisters," Camino said as he approached them.

"Hey, Camino, you don't have wings. How are you flying?" Seaspring pointed out, raising a very good question.

"I am also a spirit," he replied, then flew to the front of the pack.

"That makes so much sense," Seaspring said, her tone dripping with sarcasm.

They flew a little longer until they reached the castle gate. This one was strikingly different from the one at the Shadow of the Moon; it gleamed golden and had a friendly appearance.

As they landed, the gates swung open immediately. Walking into the expansive courtyard, they spotted a group of children playing a game near the entrance. The moment they saw Camino, they ran over to him excitedly.

"Hello, children! We're on our way to see King Amar," he said with a smile.

"Okay! See you soon, Camino!" they replied, dashing back to their game.

Upon entering the castle, they were greeted once more by a family and a guard at the door. Camino led them down a grand hallway toward the throne room.

"Ah, Camino. I was expecting you. Please come in, and welcome Allie, Amber, Stella, and Jacob. It's wonderful to see you, Seaspring, Silverspark, and Bloodwing as well." The voice was soothing and flowing, like a gentle river. Allie immediately recognized it; King Amar was the one who had spoken to her all those times.

As they entered, Allie was awestruck by the sight before her. In the center of the room stood a magnificent golden throne, upon which sat King Amar, the great lion. His mane and fur shimmered with a warm glow, and his eyes were the most beautiful she had ever seen. In that moment, Allie felt an undeniable sense of care and love radiating from him. Realizing this, a wave of peace and healing washed over her.

"Come forward, Allie. You have been healed. Try to shapeshift," he said gently.

Allie hesitated, then focused. *Turn into a tigar.* To her surprise, it worked. *Turn into myself.*

"It worked! But you said you had healed me," she exclaimed, astonished.

Allie felt a wave of confusion.

"I know. You've been healed of the enchantment. However, I have great things in store for you, and I leave you with this gift to fulfill my plans," he explained.

Allie was left speechless.

"You're welcome, child," he laughed warmly. "Now, Amber, you've told them about the magic in this world, haven't you?"

"Yes, sir. I have," Amber replied, looking down.

"This magic is very real, though it may not be what you expect. They are gifts. Amber, your 'super strength,' as you call it, is a reflection of your trust in me. You may not remember, but in your old world, you knew me by a different name. Your strength and bravery at heart are amplified in this realm through your 'super strength.' Allie, your compassion to see through others' eyes is expressed through shapeshifting. Stella, your gentleness, and Jacob, your intelligence, will guide both of you to discover your gifts."

Amber, Stella, Jacob, and Allie exchanged uncertain glances. Stella glanced down at her arm, still wrapped by Sage, knowing it remained cut open from the brief battle at Crescent Fortress.

"Sir, can you—" Stella began, nodding toward her arm.

"You have everything you need," King Amar replied simply.

Allie looked at Stella, confusion evident in her expression. Stella nodded uncertainty, glancing down at her arm as she continued to hold it.

Jacob gasped. "Stella, look at your arm!"

"I know. It looks so bad..." She paused abruptly. Allie turned to her, curious about why she had stopped speaking.

The cut on Stella's arm began to close, and soon it was completely healed, as if the battle had never happened!

"Thank you!" Stella exclaimed, turning to King Amar.

"It wasn't me; that was you, Stella."

"Me?" she questioned, surprised. King Amar simply smiled.

"The realm you just left, the one you call the Pertiaus Realm, is a reflection of evil on Earth. It is considered the true realm, while your world—Earth—is known as Illusion. For that is what it is: an illusion of what truly exists, even though Earth feels very real."

"This realm, the Cielo Realm, is what will come. This is where you belong; this is your future home."

Slowly, the pieces began to fall into place, confirming what Sephtis had told them.

"Long ago, I created your world, but Sephtis, one of my greatest generals, sought the throne for himself. So he descended into Illusion. Yes, he is there, even though you can't see him. Sephtis uses his Blood Rippers to ravage that land, too proud to face it himself. He claims the title of king over both that world and the Pertiaus Realm." King Amar stepped down from his throne.

"And now, we celebrate."

Chapter 18

As Allie looked around at her friends' faces, she saw understanding reflected in their eyes, as if all the pieces of the puzzle were finally falling into place. Just then, Camino nuzzled her leg, offering silent support

"Are you satisfied with your findings, Allie?" Camino asked.

"Yes, thank you, Camino," she replied with a smile.

They stepped into the main hall of the castle alongside Camino and King Amar. Amber watched them as they walked, curiosity shining in her eyes.

"I just realized something! When Sephtis cast the spell on the portal that pulled my parents out of the world, I didn't go because I was full of magic!" she exclaimed, her eyes wide with revelation.

When they reached the courtyard, a crowd awaited them—humans and creatures of all kinds. Their group dispersed, engaging in conversations with the inhabitants of the Cielo Realm. In just a few hours, Allie's entire life and path changed drastically. It was something she hadn't expected, but it was a change she wouldn't trade for anything.

The courtyard was decorated like a fiesta, with a table laden with food off to the side and music drifting down from what seemed to be the sky. Allie and Stella approached the food table, where Lila was introducing them to some of her friends. Meanwhile, Jacob led Amber over to a group of teenagers playing basketball.

The party went on for a long time, and as darkness began to settle, Allie and Stella bumped into Amber and Jacob.

"I'm going to grab some food—playing basketball made me hungry. See you guys! And watch out for Straightshot here," Jacob said with a grin before heading off.

"Who's Straightshot?" Stella asked.

Amber laughed. "That's the nickname all the boys gave me. They taught me how to play basketball, and I ended up beating them all in, like, five minutes!"

They all laughed, and Allie wished this moment could last forever.

But Camino approached her again. Allie stepped to the side to talk to him.

"You know you will be leaving soon," he said gently.

"What! No! I thought King Amar said this was my home," she replied, concern flooding her voice.

"Yes, King Amar was not lying; this is your home. But you must fulfill his plans in your world first. In King Amar's time, you will return here again—perhaps even more than once," Camino said before walking off toward Jacob.

Allie couldn't believe they were going to leave soon. It felt like they had just arrived, yet it already felt like home. Just then, Amber approached her.

"Did Camino tell you?" Amber asked, tears glistening in her eyes.

"Yes..." Allie replied softly.

"Allie, Amber, come here, please," King Amar called in his soothing, deep voice.

As they approached him, Stella joined them, and soon they all stood together before King Amar.

"As I'm sure Camino has told you, you will be leaving soon," King Amar said.

"Yes, King Amar, but may we ask why? We have completed the mission you assigned to us here," Amber stated confidently.

"You may have completed what I asked of you here, child, but I have more in store for you in the days to come. I need you back on Earth. You are strong, and I still need your help to guide others there." King Amar then turned his attention to Allie.

"Allie, the enchantment Sephtis placed upon you is gone. You still possess your shapeshifting powers, but you will unlock even more when you look to me. All of you will." Allie didn't fully understand him, but she trusted him nonetheless.

"Stella, remember to be kind to all. Love everyone, even your enemies." With that, King Amar walked further into the courtyard, and they followed.

"People and creatures of all nations, I welcome you to bid farewell to your friends—Amber, Allie, Stella, and Jacob. But do not fret, for they will return." As King Amar finished addressing the crowd, Jacob stepped forward.

"Son, don't let your heart and mind fall to the dark," King Amar said kindly.

Jacob nodded and joined them, along with the crowd. People they had just met, as well as familiar faces, came together for a bittersweet farewell. Allie spotted Lila, the kind old woman who had welcomed them, and she also recognized the children from the courtyard.

Allie approached Silverspark and wrapped her arms around her neck.

"I'm leaving soon. I'm going back home. Camino told me," she said slowly, her heart heavy.

"No, Allie! I can't let you go," Silverspark said, resting her head on Allie's back.

"I know. But we have to trust King Amar." Just then, King Amar approached them.

"Trust me, for I have a purpose for this departure," he said gently to Silverspark. She nodded, though tears still filled her eyes.

Allie looked up to see Stella and Amber in a similar embrace with Bloodwing and Seaspring.

She noticed Jacob standing there as the others said their goodbyes to their dragons. Her heart ached for him; his dragon, DarkIce, had turned out to be a traitor and the second-in-command of Sephtis.

She walked over to him. "Hey, I'm sorry about DarkIce," Allie said gently.

"It's okay. I just hope he chooses to accept the light," Jacob replied.

Once Stella and Amber had said their goodbyes to their dragons, they all gathered in the courtyard.

As Allie glanced into the crowd one last time, she heard goodbyes in various languages, yet she understood each one. As the world began to fade away, King Amar's voice resonated one final time:

"You will return."

Suddenly, they found themselves standing in the clearing near Allie and Jacob's house. In just seven days, Stella and Allie had met Amber, encountered the dragons, and embarked on a wild adventure. They had traveled to the Shadow of the Moon and then to the Cielo Realm, uncovered the truth, and now received an important assignment.

Deep breath.

Allie gazed up at the moon in the sky before turning to her friends.

"Welcome back to Earth, Amber."

Epilogue

"**M**om! Uncle Jacob and Aunt Amber are here!" Crystal, Allie's daughter, yelled from the door.

"Thanks, baby! You can let them in," Allie replied. "Tell them I'm in my office."

She heard chatter in the hallway, and moments later, Amber and Jacob walked in.

"Hey, guys! How are you doing?" Allie asked just as the doorbell rang again.

"Sorry I'm late! Jake got called into work last minute, and it took forever to find a babysitter for Mia and Milly. Those two are a handful!" Stella rushed in, clearly flustered. Ever since becoming a mom to twin girls three years ago, she seemed perpetually under a blanket of stress.

"Well, calm down, because Amber and Jacob just got here too," Allie said, chuckling as she closed the tabs on her computer.

They often gathered to discuss life, the Realm, and King Amar, but it had been a few months since their last get-together.

As they caught up, a voice they all recognized echoed through the room.

"Come now. The Realm is in need of you." King Amar's voice rang clear.

They exchanged knowing smiles, and Amber pulled her sword from her backpack, fastening it around her waist.

Suddenly, one of the walls in Allie's office began to swirl, revealing a view of the Cielo Realm beyond.

"Mom!" Crystal called from the other room.

"Hold on, sweetie! We're about to take a little field trip," Allie smiled, excitement bubbling within her.

Note from the author

The Truth

King Amar represents the one true God and Camino is Jesus our savior. God loves us so much that he sent his Son down to die for us. That's why we celebrate Christmas and Easter.

But just like Sephtis made creatures do bad things by getting into their minds, Satan does the same thing to us.

Romans 3:10 NIV

As the Scriptures say, "No one is righteous— not even one.
Romans 3:23 NIV
For everyone has sinned; we all fall short of God's glorious standard.

But just like King Amar said that he sent Camino down to give us a way to him and the truth, God sent his one and only Son down to die for our sins and give us a way to heaven.
Romans 5:8 NIV
Romans 6:23 NIV
When Allie, Jacob, Amber, Stella, Silverpsark, Seaspring and Bloodwing all trusted King Amar and knew he was the truth and filled their hearts with his truth, he said they were saved. That they were new creations and that the Cielo Ream was home.
Romans 10:9-10 NIV

If you openly declare that Jesus is Lord and believe in your heart that God raised him from the dead, you will be saved.

Romans 10:13 NIV

For "Everyone who calls on the name of the LORD will be saved."

God, King Amar, wants you to be his child. He loves you enough to let his Son die for you. God gave you a way to have eternal life with him through Jesus Christ! How amazing is that! He loves you. He always will, and he always has. Let him come into your heart, and change your life, just like King Amar did for Allie and the others.

And to all who are God's disciples he gives them this commandment just as King Amar did.

Matthew 28:19 NIV

Go. Share God's love with the world and let his truth change your life as well.

His Grace Alone,
Zoey Daly